The Adventure of
the Secret Necklace
and Other Stories

The Adventure of the Secret Necklace and Other Stories

The Adventure of the Secret Necklace

Enid Blyton

Illustrations by Mark Robertson

Mischief at St Rollo's

Enid Blyton

Illustrations by Judith Lawton

The Boy Who Wanted a Dog

Enid Blyton

Illustrations by Gareth Floyd

BLOOMSBURY
CHILDREN'S
BOOKS

First published by Parragon Publishing in 1999
Queen Street House, 4/5 Queen Street, Bath BA1 1HE

The Adventure of the Secret Necklace was first
published by Lutterworth Press in 1954
Mischief at St Rollo's was first published by T. Werner Laurie Ltd in 1947
The Boy Who Wanted a Dog was first published by Lutterworth Press
in 1963
First published by Bloomsbury Publishing Plc in 1997
38 Soho Square, London, W1V 5DF

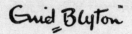

ISBN 1 84164 092 1

Printed in Scotland by Caledonian International Book Manufacturing Ltd

10 9 8 7 6 5 4 3 2 1

Cover Design by Mandy Sherliker

Contents

The Adventure of the Secret
    Necklace   11

Mischief at St Rollo's   101

The Boy Who Wanted a Dog   213

The Adventure of
the Secret Necklace

The Adventure of
the Secret Necklace

Enid Blyton
Illustrations by Mark Robertson

BLOOMSBURY
CHILDREN'S
BOOKS

Contents

1 An Exciting Letter   17

2 All the Way to Granny's   23

3 Cousin Ralph   29

4 At Granny's   35

5 Before Breakfast   41

6 Ralph Gets into Trouble   47

7 The End of the Day   53

8 Granny Sets a Few Puzzles   59

9 The Old, Old Book   65

10 A Quarrel   71

11 In the Middle of the Night   77

12 The Hidey-Hole   83

13 The End of the Adventure   89

CHAPTER 1

AN EXCITING LETTER

'Ding-ding-ding-a-ding!' A bell jingled loudly downstairs, and there was a scurry and a yell from upstairs.

'Bob! There's the breakfast bell! Can you do my dress up at the back for me? Quick!'

Bob went to his twin sister, Mary. 'Why do girls have dresses that do up at the back?' he grumbled. 'I hate all these hooks and things.'

'There are only two,' said Mary. 'Hurry, Bob, we'll be late!'

Bob hurried, and the hooks went into the eyes neatly. Then both children raced downstairs and into the breakfast-room. Daddy was just about to sit down.

'Ha! It's you, is it?' he said. 'I had a feeling it was an elephant or two crashing down the stairs. You're just in time.'

The twins kissed their mother and father and

sat down to their breakfast. Mary's sharp eyes caught sight of a letter on her mother's plate.

'You've got a letter,' she said, 'and I know who it's from. It's from Granny! I always know her big, spidery writing. Open it, Mummy. Perhaps she is coming to stay with us.'

Mummy opened the letter and read it. 'No – she's not coming to stay,' she said. 'But she wants *you* to go! Would you like to?'

'Oh *yes*!' said both twins together. They had only once been to stay with Granny, when they were very tiny, because she lived rather a long way away – but they remembered her old, old house with its strange corners and windows.

'When can we go?' asked Bob. 'As soon as we break up school? I'd like to see Granny again. She's strict, isn't she – but she's kind too. I like her.'

'I *love* her,' said Mary. 'I love her twinkly eyes, and her pretty white hair – and I don't mind her being strict a bit, so long as I know what she's strict about. I mean, she tells us what she doesn't like us to do, so we *know*. Can we go soon?'

'Granny says as soon as school ends, you may go to her,' said Mummy, reading the letter again. 'And one of the reasons she wants you is that she will have another child staying there – and she thinks it would be very nice for him to have your company – somebody to play with.'

'Oh,' said Bob, not quite so pleased. 'I thought we would be having Granny to ourselves. Who's the other boy?'

'Your cousin Ralph – you've never seen him,' said Mummy. 'Your granny is *his* granny too, because his daddy is brother to your daddy, and Granny is their mother.'

The twins worked this out. 'Oh yes,' said Mary. 'We've never seen Ralph. Why haven't we?'

'Only because your uncle John, his daddy, has had to travel about all over the place, taking his wife and child with him,' said Daddy, looking up from his paper. 'Very bad for the boy – no proper schooling, no proper home. You two will be good for him.'

The twins didn't feel as if they wanted to be 'good for him'. It made them sound like medicine or stewed apples or prunes – things that were always 'good for you'.

'How old is Ralph?' asked Bob, hoping he wouldn't be much older than he was.

'Let me see – you're seven – and Ralph is almost a year older – he'll be about eight,' said Mummy. 'I've no idea what he's like, because your uncle and aunt have been out of the country for two years now, and they never send any photographs. I expect he will enjoy having two cousins to play with.'

The twins got on with their breakfast. They weren't quite sure about Ralph – but when they began to think about Granny, and her old house, and the big garden with its fruit trees and flowers, they smiled secretly at one another.

'Lovely!' thought Mary. 'It's fun to go and stay in a new place.'

'Fine!' thought Bob. 'I wonder if that little pony is still at Granny's – we were too little to ride him last time – but this time we could. And I hope Jiminy the dog is still there. I liked old Jiminy.'

There was only one more week of school to go. When the last day came, the twins raced home. 'Mummy! Where are you? We've got some good news!'

'What is it?' said Mummy, looking up from her mending.

'We're top of our class – *both* top together, Bob and I!' shouted Mary. 'Isn't that a surprise?'

'Well, you've worked hard,' said Mummy, simply delighted. 'I really *am* proud of you. Dear me, to think I am one of the lucky mothers whose children work hard enough to be top!'

Daddy was pleased too. 'I shall give you each five pounds,' he said. 'You can take it to spend when you are away at Granny's.'

Five pounds! What a lot of money that seemed! Bob and Mary at once thought of ice-creams by the dozen, bars of chocolate, toffees and books and new crayons.

'Only two days more and we go to Granny's,' said Bob, putting his money carefully into a little leather purse. 'We're lucky – top of our form – five pounds each – and a lovely holiday at Granny's!'

Only two days more – and away they would go!

CHAPTER 2
ALL THE WAY
TO GRANNY'S

The twins helped their mother to pack their clothes in a small trunk. 'It's a good thing it's summer-time,' said Mummy. 'Your things take up so little room when they are just cotton frocks and shorts and shirts.'

'Don't put in any jerseys and mackintoshes,' begged Mary. 'We shan't need those!'

Mummy laughed. 'What a thing to say! What would Granny think of me if the weather turned cold or wet, and you hadn't a single jersey or mackintosh to wear? Don't be silly, Mary!'

Bob knew why Mary had said that. The weather was so lovely just then, the sky so blue, the sun so hot that it seemed quite impossible to think of cold or rain.

'Holiday weather!' he said. 'You won't miss us *too* much, will you, Mummy?'

'Not if you are happy and having a good

time,' said Mummy. 'I'll be glad for you, you see. It will be strange without you, of course – but Granny's sweet and kind, and she will look after you well for me. Now – where did I put those sandals?'

'Here they are,' said Bob. 'Have we got to keep very very *clean* at Granny's, Mummy? Cleaner than at home?'

'Well, Granny has always said that your daddy was just about the dirtiest little boy she ever knew,' said Mummy, smiling. 'So I don't expect she'll mind if you do get a bit dirty sometimes.'

'Goodness, was Daddy *really* a dirty little boy?' said Mary, in astonishment, thinking of her big, clean, nice-smelling father, with his polished shoes and well-scrubbed hands. 'Bob – maybe one day you'll be as clean as Daddy!'

'There – that's really everything, I think,' said Mummy, shutting down the lid. 'Now, what's the time? We've got just half-an-hour to label the trunk and strap it up safely, and get you ready. I'm going to take you and your luggage to the station in the car.'

The twins got themselves ready, and then went to say goodbye to their playroom and all the things in it. Mummy had packed Bob's monkey, which he couldn't bear to leave behind, and Mary's third-best doll, Elizabeth.

'Although she's only my third-best, I love her

most of all,' Mary said. 'She's cuddly, and she's got a nice smile, and she goes to sleep beautifully. Please pack her *very* carefully, Mummy.'

At last they were on the way to the station. The porter came to get their trunk. Mummy bought the tickets and there they were, standing on the platform waiting for the train to rumble loudly into the station.

It came at last, whistling shrilly, making Mary jump. Mummy put them into a carriage. 'I'll tell the guard to come and have a look at you now and then,' she said. 'You'll be quite all right, because you don't have to change anywhere. Eat your sandwiches when you see a clock on some station pointing to half-past twelve.'

'Goodbye, Mummy!' cried both children, hugging their mother and feeling suddenly that they didn't want to leave her behind. 'We'll write to you.'

'Bob, you'll remember that brothers *always* have to take care of their sisters, won't you?' said Mummy, 'So look after Mary. Goodbye, dears, have a lovely time!'

The guard whistled and waved his green flag. The train grunted and went off again, pulling the carriages in a rumbling row. The twins leaned out of the window and waved wildly. When at last they could see the platform no longer they sat back in the carriage.

'It's awfully grown-up, going on a long journey by ourselves like this,' said Mary. 'I hope half-past twelve won't be a long time coming. I feel hungry already.'

'Goodness! It's not half-past ten yet,' said Bob. 'You can have some chocolate at eleven. Mummy gave us a bar each. What shall we do now? Look out of the window – or read our books?'

'Oh, look out of the window!' said Mary. 'Let's have half-an-hour at that, then eat our chocolate, then have a game of seeing who can count the most houses out of the window. Then we'll watch for a station clock to tell us if it's lunch-time.

The time flew by. Soon they were having their lunch, and how hungry they were. Mummy had packed up some sardine sandwiches, tomato sandwiches, big pieces of fruit cake, a banana each, and another two bars of chocolate. They ate every single thing.

The guard came along every now and again and chatted to them. He said he would be sure to tell them when they arrived at the right station.

'We'll know all right,' said Bob, rather grandly. 'We'll be looking out ourselves.'

But, you know, they weren't! They both fell fast asleep after their lunch, and didn't wake up till the guard came along, shouting 'Curlington Junction! Curlington!'

He put his head in at their window. 'Hey! You there! Wake up, and get out quickly! I've got a porter for your luggage, and he's taking the trunk out of my van.'

Goodness! The twins almost fell out of the carriage in their hurry – and there, not far away, standing on the platform anxiously looking for them, was Granny!

She saw them at once and ran to them, hugging them both at once.

'Bob! Mary! Here you are at last, darlings! I've been so looking forward to seeing you. Come along – I've got the pony-trap outside, waiting. We'll soon be home.'

Out of the station they went – and there, in the little cart, was the pony they used to know. What a lovely beginning to a holiday!

CHAPTER 3

COUSIN RALPH

The porter brought out the small trunk that the children had with them, and stowed it in the pony-cart. Bob and Mary went to pet the small chestnut pony.

'Hello, Bonny! Do you remember us?' asked Bob. 'You're fatter, Bonny! Mary, he remembers us!'

'Of course he does,' said Granny, getting into the little pony-cart and sitting down. 'He hopes you are old enough to have a ride on him this time. Ralph rides him quite a lot.'

'Where *is* Ralph?' asked Mary, climbing into the little cart too. 'Why didn't he come with you to meet us, Granny?'

'I told him to,' said Granny, 'but when I was ready to start he was nowhere to be seen. He's probably stalking Red Indians or looking for spies, or ambushing bandits.'

'Oh,' said Mary. This sounded rather good. The twins liked playing at Red Indians themselves!

'Is Ralph nice?' Mary asked Granny.

'Well, now, I wouldn't tell you he wasn't, would I?' said Granny, cracking her whip a little to make Bonny go a little faster. 'You wait and see. You're all my grandchildren, and I'm fond of every one of you. Get up, there, Bonny, you're very slow today! Surely you don't mind two or three in the cart and a small trunk!'

Bonny trotted on, flinging his head into the air every now and again. His little hooves made a merry clip-clopping noise. The children felt very happy.

'I do like the beginnings of things,' said Mary, suddenly. 'The beginnings of a holiday – the beginnings of a pantomime – the beginnings of a picnic. I wish beginnings lasted longer.'

'They'd be middles then!' said Bob. 'Granny, will it be tea-time when we get home with you? I feel as if it might be.'

Granny laughed. 'Oh yes, it will be tea-time – with new bread and my own strawberry jam – and honey from my own bees – and a chocolate sponge cake made by Cookie – you remember her, don't you? And some of those chocolate biscuits you like so much.'

'Oh! Fancy your remembering that we like chocolate biscuits!' said Mary, pleased. 'You really are a proper granny.'

That made Granny laugh again. 'Oh, I'm a proper granny all right, so just mind your P's and Q's!' she said, with a twinkle in her eye. 'Now – here we are. Welcome to Tall Chimneys!'

That was the strange name of Granny's old house, and it suited it very well, because its chimneys were very tall indeed – old, old chimneys made of red brick like the house itself.

'I like your house, Granny,' said Mary. 'It looks old and friendly and – well, rather mysterious too. As if it had quite a lot of secrets.'

'It probably has,' said Granny, getting down. 'It's a few hundred years old, you know. Now, here comes Mr Turner to take the trunk. We'll go in.'

'Hello, Mr Turner!' called Bob. 'I remember you! And oh – here's Jiminy! Jiminy, do you remember us?'

A black spaniel ran up to them, barking a welcome. The children fell on him at once. 'Jiminy! You're just the same – but *you're* a bit fatter too! Your tongue's just as licky. Granny, he's licked my face all over.'

'Then I suppose you won't think it needs washing, but it does!' said Granny. 'Take the trunk up to the corner bedroom, Mr Turner, and then take Bonny to the stables. I shan't want him any more today.'

Turner, big and strong, lifted the trunk as if it were nothing but a box of chocolates, and ran up the stairs with it. The children went indoors, with Jiminy leaping round them in delight.

'Do you know the way up to your room?' asked Granny. 'You remember? Very well, go up now, and just wash your faces and hands. You'll find a comb there for your hair.'

The twins ran up the big, curving staircase. They remembered the little corner bedroom, with its slanting ceiling – lovely!

'Here it is,' said Bob, running in. Then he stopped suddenly. A loud fierce voice sounded from somewhere nearby.

'Spies! I know you! Put your hands up or I'll shoot!'

There was a loud *bang* as if a shot had gone off. Mary gave a scream and clung to Bob. Then the door of a cupboard was flung open and out stalked a big boy, dressed in cowboy things. He grinned at them.

'Did I scare you? I hope I did! I'm Ralph!'

The twins stared at him. 'What was that bang?' said Mary, her heart still beating fast.

'A paper bag! I blew it up and popped it to make you think it was a shot!' said Ralph, grinning. 'I'm glad you've come. It's awfully dull here. You look rather small, though – only just little kids. That's a pity.'

'We're seven,' said Bob, 'so we're *not* little kids. You're not much older yourself, anyway.'

'I'm bigger, though – much bigger,' said Ralph. And indeed he was. He grinned and stamped out of the room. The twins looked at each other.

Were they going to like him – or weren't they? They felt very doubtful indeed!

CHAPTER 4

AT GRANNY'S

The twins washed their hands and went down to tea. As Granny had said, it was a very fine tea. Bob and Mary sat down, looking at the well-spread table in delight.

Ralph came in, and sat down too. He smiled cheekily at his grandmother. 'I'm sorry I wasn't about when you went,' he said. 'I forgot the time.'

'I didn't really expect you,' said Granny. 'Will you please go and wash your hands and face, Ralph, and take your cowboy hat off? I've told you that before.'

'I'll just take my hat off,' said Ralph, and threw it on the floor. Then he reached out for the bread-and-butter.

'You heard what I said, Ralph,' said Granny. 'No tea unless you come properly washed and tidied. Don't let me have to find fault with you in the first few minutes your cousins are here!'

Ralph scowled. He gave the table leg a kick, got up and went out of the room. He certainly didn't like being scolded in front of his small cousins!

'Ralph is very big for his age, isn't he?' said Mary, making herself a fine strawberry jam sandwich. 'This *is* lovely jam, Granny – just as nice as Mummy makes at home.'

'That's good,' said Granny. 'Yes, Ralph *is* big for his age – but I expect you'll find that you know much more than he does. You can teach him a lot.'

This sounded rather surprising to Bob and Mary. 'Can't he read then – or do sums?' she asked.

'He only reads comics, not books,' said Granny, 'and that's a pity. He's not *very* good at sums, either – but that's not quite what I meant. Anyway, you'll soon find out. He's a good boy at heart and I'm very fond of him. He'll soon shake down and be sensible, now you've come.'

Mary hoped that he would! She hadn't forgotten the fright she had had when he had yelled from the cupboard, burst the paper bag, and flung himself out suddenly into their bedroom.

Ralph came down looking clean and cheerful. He made a simply enormous tea, and had to go out and ask for more bread-and-butter and honey.

'You'll have to grow more corn for bread, keep more cows for butter, and more bees to make honey, if you have us all staying here for long!' said Mary to her grandmother. That made them all laugh.

'Now, if you've finished, you can go,' said Granny. 'Ralph, take the twins and show them everything. They will have forgotten the way round the garden and into the farmyard.'

'Right,' said Ralph. 'Just half a minute.'

He raced upstairs, two steps at a time. He came down again in a few minutes, dressed as a Red Indian, with a magnificent tail of feathers falling from his head-dress to his feet. He really looked very grand. He had a rubber axe in his belt, and had daubed his face with coloured chalk.

'Good gracious!' said Granny. 'I shall never get used to your face looking like that!'

'You look fine,' said Bob, wishing he had a Red Indian suit like Ralph's. 'Come on – let's go out. I want to see round the garden again.'

Once out in the garden Ralph acted like a real Red Indian, startling Mary very much. He stalked beside a hedge, bent double, and then, at the end of it, leapt high into the air with a tremendous yell, flourishing his axe.

A scream came from the other side of the hedge, and then an angry voice.

'I've told you before not to jump at me like that, Ralph! Here I am, picking peas, and you've made me upset the whole basket. You come and pick the pods up for me!'

'No, thanks!' said Ralph, and stalked on, his eye on Turner, who had just appeared out of a shed.

Mary stopped by Cookie. 'I'll pick up the pods,' she said. 'Oh goodness – Ralph has pounced on Mr Turner now!'

There was a loud yell as Ralph leapt on Turner – and then another as Turner, startled, swung round and flung him off roughly. Ralph hit the ground hard, and sat up, dazed. To the twins' amazement he began to howl.

'You hurt me! You've no right to fling me about like that. I'll tell my grandmother!'

'So will I,' said Turner, grimly, and went back into the shed again. 'Cry-baby!'

Ralph got up, took a look at the twins, who stood near by feeling ashamed of him, and then ran off round a corner.

'Well, he may be big, but he's not very brave,' said Mary. 'Come on, let's go round the garden alone.'

So they went round it, peeping into corners they remembered, dabbling in the goldfish pond, looking up into a tree they used to climb, watching the ducks on the duck-pond. They

looked for eggs in the hen-house, and all the time Jiminy came round with them, his stump of a tail wagging hard.

'Everything's lovely!' said Mary. 'We'll ride Bonny tomorrow – and ask Granny if we can pick some of those ripe plums for her – and climb that tree!'

'I wish Ralph wasn't staying here too,' said Bob – and then he jumped. A voice came from behind a nearby bush.

'I heard what you said! Mean things! You're just two silly little kids!' And out leapt Ralph, flourishing his rubber axe. Oh dear – what a pity he had heard what Bob had said!

CHAPTER 5

BEFORE BREAKFAST

It was lovely to wake up the next morning and see the sun streaming in at the leaded panes of their bedroom window. The twins stared out happily. They could see a long way, over hills and fields and valleys. They could see lazy cows in the fields, and white sheep dotted about the hills.

'It's going to be a lovely day,' said Mary. 'Oh blow – there's Ralph!'

Ralph had the room next door. He was getting up and sounded as if he were pulling open all the drawers, moving half the furniture, and dropping dozens of things on the floor. He certainly was a very noisy boy!

He suddenly gave a tremendous rap on their door and yelled loudly: 'Come on, lazy-bones! Buck up! It's half-past seven.'

He then flung open the door. He was now dressed as a sailor, in long blue trousers, wide at

41

the ankles, a blue shirt with a big sailor collar, and a sailor hat. He saluted smartly and grinned.

'However many fancy-dresses have you got?' asked Mary.

Ralph stopped smiling, and gave a scowl. 'They're not fancy-dresses. They're the real thing, only made my own size. Fancy-dresses! You don't know what you are talking about!'

He slammed the door and was gone. 'Goodness!' said Mary. 'What a boy! Come on, let's get up and go out. It's a heavenly day.'

They were soon out in the garden. They helped Cookie to feed the hens, and then took some bread to feed the ducks. A small pebble whizzed by Bob's ankles and into the pond with a splash. He turned round.

Ralph was near by, still in his sailor suit, laughing. He threw another pebble and it hit a duck on the back, making it scurry over the pond quacking.

'Don't do that,' said Mary, at once. That was a silly thing to say to Ralph, of course. He at once picked up a bigger stone and threw it into the pond, making the ducks swim away to the sides at once.

'Look here,' said Bob, stepping right up to Ralph, who was quite a head taller than he was. 'Look here, you are NOT to throw stones at the ducks. That's a mean thing to do – to hurt creatures that have never done you any harm.'

'Pooh!' said Ralph, and bent to pick up another stone. Someone leapt on him fiercely, and he fell face downwards to the ground. He felt slaps

on each side of his face and yelled loudly.

'I'll tell Granny on you, Bob! Getting me down like this! You bully! I'll tell Granny!'

He managed to get up, and glared at his attacker – and dear me, what a surprise he got! It wasn't Bob who had leapt at him and slapped him – it was Mary! A very small and angry Mary, her cheeks red, her eyes bright and hard.

'It wasn't Bob,' she said. 'It was *me*, Mary! It served you right for throwing stones at the ducks. Come along and we'll tell Granny I knocked you over and slapped you. Come on, I don't mind.'

But Ralph wasn't going to tell anyone that a small girl had attacked him and slapped him – nor was he going to tell the reason why. He went very red and looked ashamed.

'I wasn't *really* stoning the ducks,' he said. 'I only meant to startle them – they're silly creatures, anyway.'

'Well, I'll slap you again if you try any more tricks like that!' said Mary, who was never afraid to stick up for anything smaller or weaker than herself. 'Or Bob will. You're a coward! You think yourself so big and grand, dressing up and acting like a Red Indian, or a cowboy or something – and you're really just a nasty little boy and a cry-baby!'

A bell rang out. Ralph gave a feeble smile and

brushed himself down. 'All right, all right, Miss Sharp-Claws. There's the breakfast bell. We'll have to go in.'

Granny didn't know that anything had happened before breakfast, and nobody told her. They all ate their cornflakes and boiled eggs and bread and butter, and chattered away to Granny.

'I thought we would take Bonny and the pony-cart and go down to the river this morning,' said Granny. 'We could take a picnic lunch with us – and you can paddle, if you like.'

'Ooooh – let's!' said Mary, delighted. Ralph took up a spoon and banged it on the table, making Granny jump.

'Fine! GRAND!' he shouted. 'I'm a sailor today, and I want to get near water. Hurrah!'

'That's enough, Ralph,' said Granny. 'Put that spoon down. You're not a baby now!'

'We could have a swim!' said Bob. 'Oh Granny, it's a lovely idea of yours!'

The twins ran off in excitement after breakfast. Where were their swim-suits? Granny had unpacked for them and put them into one of the drawers. They found them and were just going downstairs when they ran into Ralph. He looked gloomy.

'What's up?' said Bob. 'Hurry, because the pony-cart is at the door already.'

'I don't want to go,' said Ralph. 'It's a silly

idea of Granny's. Let's not go.'

'But you *wanted* to!' said Bob, in surprise. 'Don't you remember how you banged the spoon on the table? Why have you changed your mind?'

Granny's voice came up the stairs. 'Come along, all of you. We're just starting. Hurry up now!'

CHAPTER 6

RALPH GETS
INTO TROUBLE

Bonny the pony was ready with the little pony-cart. They all got in, and Granny put the picnic-basket down at their feet.

'I'll drive,' said Ralph, who still looked rather gloomy. He picked up the whip, jerked the reins and they set off down the drive.

'Don't jerk Bonny's head like that,' said Granny. 'There's no need to.'

Bonny trotted merrily out of the gate and into the lane. He slowed down when he came to the hill, and Ralph cracked the whip. Bonny didn't hurry, and he flicked the little pony, making him jump.

'Give me the reins,' said Granny, at once. 'You pretend you've ridden so many horses, Ralph, but you don't even know how to treat a willing little pony pulling four people up a hill. Here, Mary – you drive him.'

Mary took the reins, and Bonny felt the difference in handling at once. He went well up the hill, and then Bob had a turn. Ralph sat looking gloomy again, kicking his foot against the side of the cart.

'Cheer up, Ralph,' said Granny. 'You look like one of my hens left out in the rain.'

That made them all laugh. Ralph cheered up and began to boast. 'I've been up in an aeroplane,' he said to the twins. 'I bet *you* haven't! And I've been on the biggest liner in the world! And I've seen the Niagara Falls crashing down like thunder. One of these days I'm going to go over those falls in a boat. I've seen real Red Indians – and chased them too. And I've . . .'

'Keep to the truth, Ralph,' said Granny. 'We all know you've travelled a great deal – but we none of us believe that you ever chased Red Indians.'

'Look – there's the river away across those fields!' said Mary, in delight. 'Isn't it blue? How long will it take us to get to it, Granny?'

'About twenty minutes,' said Granny. 'Dear me, where is my sunshade? I didn't think the sun would be so hot. You *will* enjoy a paddle, my dears!'

'We've brought our swim-suits,' said Bob. 'Daddy taught us to swim last year. I can do breast-stroke, side-stroke and backstroke, Granny.'

'Well done!' said Granny. 'What can *you* do, Ralph?'

'Oh, I can do all those, and the crawl too. Easy!' said Ralph. 'I can swim under water as well. I swam under longer than anyone else last year. I can life-save too.'

'Well, you are big and strong,' said Granny. 'You should be able to life-save splendidly.'

'Let's paddle first,' said Mary. 'Then swim. Then have our picnic. And then could we have a boat, Granny? Rowing is easy, isn't it, Ralph?'

'Oh yes!' said Ralph. 'So is sailing. I sailed a fine big boat all by myself last year.'

'Did you really?' said Bob, impressed. 'My daddy hasn't taught us sailing yet. Only rowing.'

They came to the river and settled Granny in a nice shady spot under a tree. Then they all took off their shoes and socks and paddled in the cool water. It was lovely!

'Paddling's better than swimming any day!' said Ralph suddenly. 'Let's not bother to swim.'

'Oh, but we must!' said Mary. 'I love swimming – and perhaps you could teach us the crawl, Ralph. We don't know it.'

Ralph looked gloomy again, and gloomier still when Bob went to put on his swim-suit. Then he suddenly called out: 'Goodness me – I've forgotten my swim-suit! I can't go in to swim after all – what a pity!'

'Well, look – I've brought *two* suits!' said Bob, generously. 'I thought I'd wear one this morning and another dry one this afternoon – but you can have it. It will be a bit small, that's all.'

'Oh no – I don't want to wear your suit,' said Ralph – and then he heard Granny's voice.

'For goodness' sake put on Bob's second suit!' she called. 'A swim will do you good!' So Ralph put it on, looking very cross.

They all went into the water. Ralph went in up to his waist, and stood there, shivering. Bob and Mary dived under and came up, swimming strongly and well. Granny clapped them, delighted.

'Go in, Ralph, go in!' she cried. Bob swam up behind him, dived down and caught his legs. Into the water went Ralph, right over his head. He came up spluttering and screaming:

'You'll drown me, you'll drown me!'

Bob stared at him in surprise. 'Well, swim then, silly – go on! Show us how to do the crawl.'

But Ralph merely stood there, shivering and looking miserable. Mary swam up to him and stood up. '*I* know what's the matter with you!' she said. 'You *can't* swim, Ralph! *That's* why you left your swim-suit behind. That's why you didn't want to come. Baby!'

'You horrid girl!' cried Ralph, and tried to

slap Mary. He stumbled forward, stepped into a suddenly deep place, and went under the water.

'Save him!' yelled Mary. 'It's deep here, Bob. Save him!'

So Bob had to life-save poor Ralph, and drag him to shore, kicking and howling with fright. Dear, dear, what a to-do!

'For goodness' sake, let's have lunch!' said Granny. 'And if Ralph doesn't stop howling I'll try slapping – I believe that is quite good for people who think they have been half-drowned!'

And, as you can guess, the great sailor-man was quiet at once. How the others laughed!

CHAPTER 7

THE END OF THE DAY

The picnic went off very well, once Ralph became sensible again. He certainly ate a great deal. Granny said she didn't know where he put it all!

'Now what about a boat?' said Granny, after the picnic. 'Do you want to go rowing?'

'Oh *yes*,' said Bob and Mary. Granny turned to Ralph.

'You said you knew all about rowing and sailing. *Do* you? Because I am not going to let anyone go out in a boat unless they really know about boats – especially someone who can't swim.'

'Well – I don't know *very* much,' said Ralph, going rather red.

'That's just what I thought,' said Granny. 'You stay here with me, then – and you, Bob, go to the boatman's cottage down there, and get his little boat for yourself and Mary.'

Soon the twins were rowing back to Granny. Ralph, looking fine in his sailor-boy suit, sat and watched them sulkily. *He* ought to be rowing – he was dressed as a sailor, wasn't he? And yet he couldn't swim or manage even a small boat. He felt very small.

They went back home to tea, tired out, sunburnt, and the twins very happy, though Ralph was still sulky.

'Oh, I'm quite tired with all my rowing and swimming,' said Mary, flinging herself down on the lawn after tea.

'Have a book, and read it quietly,' said Granny.

'Oooh yes – we've brought some exciting ones away with us,' said Bob, remembering. 'I'll get them. They are all about seven children who make a Secret Society and have adventures.'

He brought out three books and gave one to Ralph. 'Here you are – *Secret Seven Adventure*, he said. 'I'll lend it to you.'

'I'd rather go and climb trees,' said Ralph. But Granny wouldn't let him, so he opened the book sulkily. The other two settled into theirs, and there was a silence that Granny quite enjoyed. Then suddenly Ralph shut his book.

'I've finished it,' he said. 'Now can I go and climb trees, Granny?'

'You can't *possibly* have finished it,' said Granny. 'You know you haven't! You can't climb trees. Sit and do nothing – or read your book properly.'

'I tell you I've read it all,' said Ralph. 'I read quickly – not slowly like Mary there – she takes ages to turn a page!'

'Be quiet. I want to read,' said Bob, and Ralph said no more. Soon Granny fell asleep, and Ralph nudged Bob.

'I'm going to climb trees,' he whispered. 'I can't sit here and read any more.'

'You haven't read a word. I don't believe you *can* read!' said Bob.

'I can! I can read very difficult words – and very fast too!' said Ralph. 'Don't wake Granny. I'm off!'

And he crept away to where the trees grew in a little thicket at the bottom of the garden. Bob and Mary let him go. They were tired of him!

Granny woke up and looked at her watch. 'Good gracious! It's time for bed. Where's that boy Ralph? If he has gone to climb trees I shall be very cross.'

They all three went indoors. Ralph was not to be seen. And then, just as Bob and Mary were getting undressed, yells came from down the garden.

'Help! Help! Come and help me!'

Bob pulled on his shirt again and tore down the stairs, with Mary following him. They went to the bottom of the garden, where the yells came from. Turner was there as well, grinning all over his face.

'*Here's* a clever boy!' he said. 'Climbs trees like a monkey – and then is afraid to get down! No one is going to climb up to you – so come on down!'

'Fetch a ladder!' called Ralph. 'I've torn my sailor shirt already. Get me a ladder.'

But Turner wouldn't – and in the end Ralph had to slither down by himself, scratching his hands, and tearing his trousers as well as his shirt. Granny was very cross with him when at last he came in.

'Go and have a bath – and tomorrow please put on an ordinary pair of shorts and a shirt,' she said. 'Wait till you are braver and more sensible, before you parade about as a Red Indian, or cowboy or sailor!'

Poor Ralph went to bed without any supper. He said he couldn't eat any because he felt sick, but Bob was sure it was because he couldn't bear to be scolded in front of the twins.

It was a nice supper too – stuffed eggs and jam tarts to follow. Mary was most surprised to see that Bob had taken two stuffed eggs and four jam tarts. How greedy!

But he had one of the eggs and two of the tarts for Ralph! Ralph was silly and he didn't like him, but Bob knew how horrid it is to go without supper. It is such a very long time till breakfast if you don't have supper.

Ralph was surprised and very grateful. 'Oh *thanks*!' he said. 'You *are* a friend. I say – it looks as if it's going to rain tonight, doesn't it? What a shame! I don't want to stay indoors all day.'

'Oh, it may be fine again tomorrow,' said Bob. 'Goodnight – and don't dream about swimming, or you'll wake up drowning!'

He went off to his room and looked out of the window. It was pouring with rain. Bother. It would be so dull staying indoors all day. But it wasn't dull. It turned out to be really very exciting!

CHAPTER 8

GRANNY SETS A
FEW PUZZLES

The next day was dark and rainy. The sun was hidden behind thick clouds, and Granny wondered what to do with the children.

'I'll set you a few puzzles,' she said. 'And the prize shall be a box of chocolates. Here's the first puzzle. Go into the dining-room, and have a good look round. Count all the clawed feet you can see there, and come back and tell me the number. Then I'll set you a few more puzzles.'

'Oh, I know *four* clawed feet there!' said Ralph. 'The stuffed fox!'

'Don't give things away!' said Mary. They went into the dining-room and looked around. Yes – stuffed fox – and a stuffed hawk with clawed feet. And a picture of an owl, he had clawed feet too.

Bob noticed a little statue of a lion on the

mantelpiece – four more clawed feet. He wondered if the others would notice it.

A bell rang after a time. That was to say they were to come back and report to Granny. 'Well,' she said, when they arrived. 'How many clawed feet did *you* see, Ralph?'

'I bet I got the most!' said Ralph. 'I counted twelve – fox, owl, hawk and lion!'

'I got those twelve too,' said Bob.

'I got *forty-four* clawed feet!' said Mary, almost crowing in delight.

'You didn't!' said Ralph. 'What are they?'

'Lion, fox, owl, hawk – and the table has four clawed feet, and so have each of the chairs, and the sideboard!' said Mary.

'Right!' said Granny. 'They are old chairs and table – the kind that have carved legs holding a ball in the claws of the foot. Well done, Mary.'

'Jolly good!' said Bob. 'What's the next puzzle, Granny?'

'Go into the drawing-room and count all the roses you can see,' said Granny. So off they ran.

'Fourteen roses in that vase – and sixteen in this one – and a rose embroidered on that cushion – and another on the fire-screen,' thought Mary. 'Any on the carpet? No. Any on the curtains? No!'

They were soon back again. 'Mary, how many?' said Granny.

'Thirty-two,' said Mary.

'Thirty-one,' said Ralph, who had counted the ones in the vases wrongly.

'*Sixty*-two!' said Bob, proudly. And he was right! 'I looked up at the ceiling, Granny, and it had roses carved on it,' he explained. Granny nodded.

'Yes – those roses were carved long ago. You were clever to notice them. Now – one last puzzle. In the gallery upstairs there are portraits of six women who lived in the olden days – great-great-great-grandmothers of yours and mine. In five of their pictures appears the same thing. I want you to tell me what it is.'

The children ran off to the gallery. It was dark up there and Bob switched on the lights. The big portraits looked down on them from the walls, most of them dark and dingy for they were very old. There were both men and women, and the children picked out the six women and looked at them carefully.

'I know, I know!' cried Mary and ran downstairs to Granny. The two boys stared and stared at the six pictures but all the women in them wore different dresses, different collars, different cuffs. Nothing in the pictures seemed the same. They gave it up.

'What's the answer, Mary?' asked Granny, when the boys joined them downstairs.

'The necklace!' said Mary. 'I could hardly see it in the first two portraits – but it was quite clear in the third one – and half-hidden under the collar of the fourth one – and shone out in the fifth one – but it wasn't in the sixth picture.'

'Yes. Quite right. You shall have the box of chocolates,' said Granny. 'Here it is.'

'Granny, have *you* got that old necklace?' asked Mary. 'Was it a kind of family necklace?'

'Yes, it was,' said Granny. 'It was a magnificent one, made of pearls, and each of the women who lived in this house wore it. But I can't wear it, because it disappeared about a hundred years ago.'

'How?' asked Mary, handing round the chocolates.

'Well, it's supposed to be hidden somewhere in this house,' said Granny. 'But people have looked everywhere, as you can guess – so I fear it must have been stolen. How I should have loved to wear it! It ought to go to your own mother, after me, Mary – but it will never be found now.'

'We'll look for it!' cried Bob. 'A treasure-hunt! Who's for a treasure-hunt! This very afternoon!'

'We are, we are!' shouted Mary and Ralph. Mary turned to Granny. 'Granny, is there a plan of the house anywhere?'

'There may be, in one of the old books in the

study,' said Granny. 'They haven't been opened for years, and are as dull as can be. But you *might* find a plan of the house if you can find a history of it – there should be one or two books about it.'

So, that afternoon, three excited children went to the study and began taking down the old books there. How dusty and dull they were – and what strange printing they had!

'Here's one about Granny's house, Tall Chimneys, look!' said Bob, at last. 'Now – let's see if there's a plan of the house – it might show secret passages or something. Ooooh look – there *is* a plan!'

CHAPTER 9

THE OLD, OLD BOOK

The three children bent over the old book. It was a history of Tall Chimneys, Granny's house. At the beginning of it were some strange old maps.

'This one shows the grounds,' said Bob. 'And this one shows the two farms. And this one – what's this one?'

They pored over the yellowed map. 'It's the cellars of the house!' said Mary, pointing to an oddly printed word. 'What's the next map?'

Bob turned over the page. 'This plan seems to be of the ground floor,' he said. 'Yes, look – this very room we are sitting in is marked – it says "Library". Isn't it peculiar to think that people sat in this very place, hundreds of years ago, perhaps looking at this same book!'

Mary was peering closely at the map. She had seen something strange – at least, it seemed strange to her. 'Look!' she said. 'There's a little door marked in the wall here – in the plan, see – but *I* can't see one in the real room we're in, can you?'

'Only the door we came in by – and that is marked on the plan too, in its right place,' said Bob, excited. 'Quick! Let's see if there is a secret door we haven't noticed in the wall over there!'

The walls had bookcases all round them. The children tried to move out the great shelves that hid the wall where a door was shown in the plan. But they couldn't. It really was terribly disappointing.

'Let's go and tell Granny,' said Mary.

'No. We just *might* find the door somehow and, who knows, we might find a hiding-place behind it where the necklace was put for safety – perhaps during a war or something,' said Bob, his face red with excitement.

Mary ran through the pages of the old book, hoping to find other maps. Two words suddenly caught her eye. 'Secret Passage'! It was a wonder she saw them, because they were printed in old-fashioned letters, and the letter *S* was just like *f*! She put her finger on the words at once, afraid she would lose them.

'Look – there must be something about the secret door on this page!' she said. 'I just noticed "Secret Passage"! I expect the door leads into it.

Oh dear – can we possibly read this funny old printing?'

Bob read the words out slowly. 'The – Secret – Passage was – made, er – er . . .'

Mary went on. 'Was made – when – the house – was – er, was built. The door – to it – leads – er – leads from the – library. It . . .'

'Isn't this *thrilling*!' said Bob. They read the whole page slowly – and on it were the directions for moving the big bookcase and getting at the door!

'I *say* – if we follow these directions, we can get through that door and see where the secret passage goes to!' said Bob, his eyes shining. 'What an adventure!'

They took the old book to the big bookcase. Mary tried to read the first direction, but it was so very dark in that corner that she couldn't. She gave the book to Ralph.

'Now you take the page over to the window and read out the directions to us one by one,' she said. 'That will be a help. Bob and I will do what the directions say. I remember the first one – take out the fifth book.'

'Yes – but from what shelf?' said Bob. 'Hey, Ralph! What shelf do we have to take the fifth book from? Buck up, silly! Can't you read what's printed there? We've read it out loud once already!'

'Er – the fifth book,' repeated Ralph, his eyes on the book. 'From the – er – the ninth shelf.'

'Ninth shelf. Let's count,' said Mary, and they counted. 'It's pretty high up,' she said. 'We'd better get the ladder.'

So they went to the kitchen and got the little ladder. They wouldn't tell Cookie what they wanted it for, and were really very mysterious about it!

They took it to the study – and just then the tea-bell rang. How very annoying!

'Well – we'll come back at once, after tea,' said Bob. 'Now – not a word to Granny. We'll find out simply everything and then give her a grand surprise.'

So they didn't tell Granny and talked about all sorts of other things. But just now and then Bob nudged Mary and smiled at her, and she knew what he meant. 'What fun we're going to have after tea!'

They went back to the study afterwards, and put the ladder against the ninth shelf. Bob climbed up while Mary held the ladder. Ralph watched.

'Ninth shelf,' said Bob. 'Wait a minute – I must know if the fifth book has to be taken from the right of the shelf or the left. Ralph, look up the directions and see. Take the book to the window again.'

Ralph pored over the page. Bob grew impatient. 'Oh for goodness' sake, buck up, Ralph. What does it say? Right or left?'

'Er – right,' said Ralph. 'Sorry. I lost the place.'

In excitement Bob took the fifth book from the right of the ninth shelf. He gave it to Mary. Then he put his hand into the gap left by the book, and felt about there. What would he find? A handle? A knob to turn? A lever to pull? It was too exciting for words!

CHAPTER 10

A QUARREL

'Can you feel anything there?' asked Mary. 'Quick, tell us!'

'I can't feel a thing!' said Bob, disappointed. 'Not a thing! Wait, I'll take a few more books out and see.'

He handed down a few books to Mary and then felt around at the back of the shelf again. No – there was nothing there – no knob, no handle, nothing!

'You come up and try, Mary,' said Bob, at last. He climbed down, his hands black with dust.

'Let's just count the shelves again to make sure we've got the ninth,' said Mary. They counted – and found that they had been right before. The shelf that Bob had been looking along was certainly the ninth.

Then Mary went up the ladder and felt all along the shelf, sliding the books to and fro so that she could reach. Bob moved the ladder when she could reach no further.

'Nothing!' said Mary. 'It's too disappointing for words. Ralph, have a turn.'

Ralph went up, but, of course, he couldn't find anything either! The three children looked at one another, frowning. Now what could be done?

Mary went to the window and picked up the old book, which Ralph had put down on the broad wooden sill. She read down the page – and then she gave a sudden squeal.

'It *isn't* the ninth shelf – it's the *fifth*! It says so quite clearly. And it's the fifth book we're to move, as we thought – but it's the fifth on the *left*, not the right, as you said, Ralph. Why did you tell us wrong?'

Ralph said nothing. He just scowled. Bob lost his temper and stamped his foot.

'You're mean! Yes, mean, mean, MEAN! You told us wrong so that we wouldn't find the secret door – and you meant to find it yourself when we weren't here.'

'I didn't,' said Ralph.

'You did, you did! It's just like you. You gave us wrong directions – and knew we wouldn't find the door. But we shall, see. And we'll turn you out of this study and lock the door so that you won't be here to see!'

Bob gave Ralph a rough push, but he stood his ground. 'No, don't! I want to see the secret door. I tell you I didn't mean to find it by myself without you. I tell you I . . .'

'We don't believe a word!' said Mary. 'Not a single word. You boast and you tell stories and you pretend to be so big and bold — but all the time you're mean — and a cry-baby too. We won't *let* you find the secret door with us! Go out of the room!'

'I shan't,' said Ralph. 'I'm bigger than either of you, and I won't go out. So there!'

Bob and Mary began to push and shove him and Ralph shoved back. They all fell over in a heap — and at that very moment Granny put her head in at the study door.

'What *are* you doing? Haven't you heard the bell to tell you it's bedtime? At least, it's *almost* bedtime, but I thought you'd like me to tell you a story first.'

'You tell it to Bob and Mary, Granny,' said Ralph, quickly. 'I don't want to hear one tonight.'

Bob glared at him. He knew quite well what was in Ralph's mind. He was going to find that secret door while he and Mary were listening to Granny! Just like him! But how could Bob stop him, unless he told Granny everything? And he did so want to keep it all a secret!

'Well, if you don't want to hear the story, Ralph, you can go up and run the bath-water,' said Granny, much to the twins' relief. 'I know you like doing that. But if you let it go above half-way I shall be very cross with you. I'm not going to have the bathroom swimming in water, like last week!'

Ralph went off, frowning. Now he wouldn't be able to stay in the study on his own. Still, the others would be hearing a story, and *they* wouldn't be able to do any exploring either! He cheered up a little and went to turn on the taps.

He wondered if he would have time to slip down to the study while the bath was filling.

'No, I'd better not,' he thought. 'I might get excited and forget the bath-water – and Granny might quite well tell me off if the floor gets flooded again. But I'll be sure to keep close to the others all day tomorrow, so that they can't find that secret door without me!'

Granny told the twins a story, then kissed them and sent them up to bed. 'I'll be up in a minute,' she said, 'and I'll bring your supper – bananas and cream. Begin to get undressed, and tell Ralph I'm just coming. He's probably sailing his boat in the bath.'

He was. He wouldn't speak to the twins when they came up, and they didn't speak to him either, except to say that Granny was soon coming. They were soon all in bed, eating sliced bananas and cream, with sugar all over the plate – lovely!

Granny tucked them in, said goodnight and left the twins in their room. Then she went to tuck Ralph in too.

Bob began to whisper to Mary. 'Mary, listen! If we leave everything till tomorrow it will be very difficult to find the door without Ralph being there – and I *won't* let him share in this now – so what about trying to find it tonight, when Granny is in bed?'

'Oh *yes!*' said Mary, thrilled. 'Yes, Bob! We'll keep awake till we hear Granny going to bed – and then we'll creep down to the study. Oh! *What* an adventure!'

CHAPTER 11

IN THE MIDDLE
OF THE NIGHT

Granny had some friends to see her that night. They stayed late, and it was difficult for the children to keep awake. In the end they took it in turns to keep awake for half-an-hour, sleeping soundly in between.

At last Bob, who was the one awake, heard the cars leaving the front door, and heard Granny coming upstairs. Click – click – click! That was the electric lights being turned off. Now, except for a light on the landing outside, and in Granny's room, the house was in darkness.

Bob woke up Mary. 'The visitors have gone,' he whispered. 'And Granny has come up to bed. Let's put on our slippers and dressing-gowns and go down. Granny won't hear us or see us now she's in her bedroom.'

Mary leapt out of her bed, wide awake with excitement. She switched on her torch, and put on her slippers and dressing-gown. 'My fingers are shaking!' she whispered to Bob. 'Oh Bob – isn't this thrilling?'

They went down the stairs very cautiously, and came into the big hall. The moon shone in through the window there, and lit up every corner. Mary was glad. She didn't like pitch-black shadows!

They went into the study. The moon shone through the windows there too, and showed them the ladder still up by the big bookcase. They went to it.

'Now – the fifth book on the fifth shelf, counting from the left,' said Bob. He went up the ladder, and then came down again. 'I can reach the fifth shelf easily, without using the ladder!' he said, and pushed it aside.

He took out the fifth book from the left of the fifth shelf and gave it to Mary. Then he began to feel about at the back of the gap where the book had stood. Mary stood watching him, trembling in excitement, trying to shine her torch where it would best help Bob.

He gave a little cry. 'Mary! There's something here – a sort of knob. I'm twisting it – no, it won't twist. I'll pull it – oh it's moved!'

There was a noise as he pulled the knob, and then another noise – a creaking, groaning noise. The bookcase suddenly seemed to push against

Bob, and he stepped back surprised.

The whole case was moving slowly out from the wall, leaving a small space behind it of about a foot. The knob worked some lever that pushed the bookcase forward in a most ingenious way! Mary stared, holding her breath. How strange!

'The secret door will be behind the bookcase!' said Bob, forgetting to whisper in his excitement. 'I'll squeeze behind and see if I can find it.'

He squeezed himself behind, shining his torch on the wooden panelling. Mary heard him take a sudden breath. 'Yes! it *is* here, Mary! The old, old secret door! It must be years and years since anyone went through it.'

'Can you open it?' asked Mary, her voice trembling. 'Oh Bob!'

Bob was feeling all over the small door, which appeared to be cut out of the panelling. His fingers came to a little hole and he poked his first finger through it. It touched something, and there was a click as if a latch had fallen.

The door swung open suddenly and silently in front of Bob. A little dark passage was behind, and Bob shone his torch into it. 'Mary! Come on! I've got the door open and it leads into the Secret Passage. Let's see where it goes. Come on!'

Mary squeezed herself behind the bookcase to the open door. It was no higher than her head.

Bob was already in the passage, and he held out his hand to her.

'Come on. It goes upwards here, in steep steps, behind the panelling. Hold my hand.'

It was dark and musty in the passage, and in one or two places they had to bend their heads because the roof was so low. It seemed to be a secret way behind the panelled walls of the study – but as the steps went on and on upwards Bob guessed they must now be behind the walls of some room upstairs.

The passage suddenly turned to the left, and then instead of going upwards ran level. It came to a sudden end at another door – a sturdy one this time, studded with big nails. It had a handle on the outside in the shape of a big iron ring, and Bob turned it.

The door opened into a tiny room, so tiny that it could only hold a wooden stool, a little wooden table, and a narrow bench on which there was an old, rotten blanket.

A wooden bowl stood on the table, and a tumbler made of thick glass. They could see nothing else inside the room at all.

'This is an old hidey-hole,' said Bob, almost too thrilled to speak. 'I wonder how many people have hidden here from their enemies, at one time or another? Look, there's even an old blanket left here by the last person.'

'There's no sign of the necklace,' said Mary, shining her torch round the tiny room. 'But look, Bob – what's that – in the wall there?'

'A cupboard – a very rough one,' said Bob. 'Not much more than a hole in the wall. Give me the stool, Mary. I'll stand on it and shine my torch inside!'

He stood on the stool, and peered into the hole, holding his torch to light him. He gave a cry and almost fell off the stool.

'Quick! Get up and look, Mary! Oh *quick*!'

CHAPTER 12

THE HIDEY-HOLE

Mary pushed Bob off the stool and stood on it herself, her heart beating fast in excitement. She shone her torch into the hole. At once something sparkled brilliantly, and flashed in the torchlight!

'Bob! Is it the necklace?' she cried. 'Oh *Bob*!'

'You can be the one to take it out,' said Bob. 'Be careful of it now – remember it may be worth thousands of pounds!'

Half-fearfully Mary put in her hand. She took hold of the sparkling mass, and gave a squeal.

'There are *lots* of things – not only a necklace. A bracelet – and rings – and brooches – oh, they're *beautiful*, Bob!'

'Hand them out to me one by one,' said Bob. 'Carefully now. Oh Mary – what*ever* will Granny say?'

Mary handed Bob the things – a bracelet that

shone like fire with red rubies – another one that glittered with diamonds – rings with stones of all sizes and shapes – brooches – and last of all the magnificent pearlj78

necklace that the twins had seen round the necks of the five women in the portraits! Yes – there was no doubt of it – this was the long-lost necklace!

Bob put everything in his dressing-gown pocket. It was the only place he could put them in. They felt quite heavy there!

'Now let's go and wake Granny!' he said, as Mary got off the stool. He shone his torch on the door, which had closed behind them. 'Come on, Mary. I wonder what Ralph will say when he knows we've got the jewellery!'

'I don't care *what* he says!' said Mary. 'He didn't deserve to share in our adventure because of his meanness in reading us out the wrong directions!'

Bob was trying to open the door. 'It's funny – there's no handle this side,' he said. 'I wonder how it opens?'

He pushed it, but it wouldn't move. He pulled it and shook it, but it didn't open. He kicked it, but it stayed firmly shut.

Mary suddenly felt frightened. 'I say, Bob – wouldn't it be dreadful if we couldn't get it open? Would we have to stay here for ever?'

'Don't be so silly! Somebody would find the bookcase was moved, and would explore and discover the secret door, and come up the passage and find us,' said Bob.

'But I don't want to be here all night!' wailed Mary. 'I don't like it – and my torch is getting very weak. I hope yours is all right. I don't want to be here all in the dark.'

'I shall look after you,' said Bob, firmly. 'You know that brothers always look after their sisters. Just think of all the lovely treasures we've got tonight, Mary. What about putting everything on? That will help you to pass the time.'

Mary thought that was a very good idea, and soon she was gleaming brightly as she put on brooches, bracelets, rings and necklace! The rings were too large so she had to close her hands to keep them from falling off.

'You look wonderful!' said Bob, shining his torch on Mary. 'Like a princess!'

Suddenly they heard a noise, and Mary clutched at Bob. 'What was that?' she whispered. 'Did you hear it?'

The noise came again. A kind of shuffling noise – was it somebody coming up the passage? Who could it be? Surely nobody lived in this little secret room?

The twins stood absolutely still, hardly daring to breathe – and then they heard a familiar voice.

'Hey! Bob! Mary! Are you here?'

'Ralph!' yelled the twins, feeling extremely glad to hear his voice. 'Yes, we're here – but we can't open the door from this side. Open it from your side, will you?'

Ralph turned the handle outside and the door opened! He looked in, shining his torch. When he saw Mary, sparkling and glittering in the beam of his torch, his mouth fell open in surprise. He could hardly say a word.

'Oh!' he said at last. 'So you found the necklace then! You *might* have waited for me, Bob.'

'I like *that*!' said Bob. 'You weren't going to wait for *us*, were you? You've got up in the middle of the night to come and explore all by yourself, haven't you? And you found that we were before you!'

'No. No, Bob, you're wrong,' said Ralph earnestly. 'I couldn't go to sleep tonight, because I was worried that you thought I was so mean – you thought I'd given you wrong directions on purpose –'

'Well, didn't you?' demanded Bob.

'No,' said Ralph. 'No, I didn't. You see – I'm not good at reading. I can't read at all to myself, really, unless it's very very easy – but I was ashamed to tell you I couldn't read those words in the old book – and I just said what I thought, and it was wrong, of course.'

There was silence for a minute. 'I see,' said Bob at last. 'So you didn't even read that book after tea yesterday – the one you seemed to finish so quickly. You do tell dreadful stories, Ralph.'

'I know. The thing is – I'm so big that people expect me to know a lot and I don't,' said Ralph. 'So I pretend, you see. And I was sorry tonight and I came to your room to tell you – but you were gone!'

'So you followed us,' said Mary. 'Well, I'm very glad you did, Ralph, or we'd have been here all night. I'm sorry we called you mean. We really and truly thought you read out wrong directions on purpose to stop us finding the door.'

'I'm sorry too,' said Bob, and solemnly held out his hand. The boys shook hands.

'I missed the adventure,' said Ralph, sorrowfully.

'Never mind – you came in at the end of it,' said Mary. 'Now – let's go and wake Granny!'

CHAPTER 25

THE END OF THE ADVENTURE

The three children left the tiny hidey-hole behind them, and went in single file down the secret passage. They came at last to the little secret door that led into the study, behind the bookcase.

The moon still shone through the windows and Mary's jewellery sparkled even more brilliantly. The boys thought she looked lovely!

They went quietly up the stairs to Granny's bedroom, and knocked on the door.

'Who's there?' said Granny's voice, sleepily.

'It's us – the twins and Ralph,' said Bob.

'What's the matter? Is one of you ill?' called Granny. 'Come in – the door isn't locked.'

They heard a click as Granny put on her light. They opened the door and went in, still in their slippers and dressing-gowns.

Granny looked at them anxiously, thinking

that one of them at least must be ill. She suddenly saw all the glittering jewellery that Mary had on.

'Mary! What have you got on? Where did you get all that?' she began. Then she saw the necklace. 'Mary – that necklace! Good gracious, am I dreaming, or is that the lost necklace? I *must* be dreaming!'

'You're not, Granny,' said Mary, coming close to the bed. 'It *is* the lost necklace – look, it's the same one that is painted in all those portraits – with the big shiny pearls and everything!'

'My dear child!' said Granny, in wonder, and put out her hand to touch the sparkling pearls. 'But these rings – and brooches – where *did* you find them? Sit on my bed and tell me. I can't wait to hear!'

So the three of them cuddled into Granny's soft eiderdown, and told their strange story – all about the plans in the old book – the mention of the passage and the directions for finding the secret door – and the hidey-hole where, most unexpectedly, they had found the jewellery in the little cubby-hole in the wall.

'I just can't believe it!' Granny kept saying. 'I just can't. To think it was there, in a place that every single person had forgotten through all these years! And all these other treasures too. How I wish I knew the story of why they were

hidden there – some thief, I suppose, stole them and put them in the safest place he knew – and then couldn't get to them again!'

'Will they be yours, all these things, Granny?' asked Mary.

'The necklace certainly will, because it belongs to the family,' said Granny, 'and I expect the other things will too. Look, this ruby ring is the one painted on the finger of the third woman in the gallery of pictures!'

So it was. Mary remembered it quite well. She took off all the sparkling jewellery carefully and handed it to Granny.

'That was a real adventure, wasn't it, Granny?' she said.

'It certainly was. Did you enjoy it too, Ralph?' asked Granny.

'Yes,' said Ralph, hoping that the twins wouldn't tell that he had only come in at the last. They didn't say a word. They were very sorry that Ralph *hadn't* shared all the adventure now. They felt much more kindly towards him, now they knew why he boasted and told such silly stories.

'You must go back to bed,' said Granny, at last. 'We'll talk about it all again tomorrow. It's too exciting for words!'

Everyone in the house was thrilled to hear about the midnight adventure. Cookie, who had been called by Mrs Hughes, the housekeeper, early next morning to see the bookcase out of its place, just couldn't believe it all.

'Well, well – it isn't often we have an adventure like this happening in Tall Chimneys!' she said. 'I'll have to make a special cake to celebrate it!'

So she did – and she actually made a beautiful necklace all round the cake, in white icing. It really was clever of her.

'Well, you will find the rest of your stay here rather dull, I'm afraid, after all this excitement,' said Granny, when they sat down to their lunch in the middle of the day.

'No, we shan't,' said Mary. 'We're going to have a jolly good time with Ralph – aren't we, Bob? We're going to teach him to swim, and to row – and lots of other things!'

Ralph beamed. 'Yes. I shan't need to show off and pretend then. Don't you worry, Granny – we're going to have a *grand* time here – and I expect I'll be a lot nicer than I've been before.'

'That's good news,' said Granny. 'You haven't always been nice, but I shall expect great things of you now.'

They did have a grand time together, and Ralph learnt a whole lot of things he didn't know before. The twins began to like him very much indeed.

Before they left Tall Chimneys, they all had a surprise. Granny said she wanted to give them goodbye presents.

'This is for you, Mary,' she said, and gave the little girl a small sparkling brooch that had been in the lost jewellery. 'I've had it cleaned and altered – and now it is just right for a little girl like you to wear at a party.'

She turned to the boys. 'And I've sold a little of the jewellery I didn't want to keep,' she said, 'and I have bought these watches, one for each of you – just to remind you of the adventure you had at Granny's!'

She gave them two splendid watches, and they put them on proudly. What would the boys at school say when they saw *those*?

'Thank you, Granny!' said the children, and hugged her. 'We've had a simply lovely time – and we never never *will* forget our Adventure of the Secret Necklace.'

Mischief at
St Rollo's

Mischief at
St Rollo's

Enid Blyton
Illustrations by Judith Lawton

BLOOMSBURY
CHILDREN'S
BOOKS

Contents

1	A New School	107
2	Settling Down	117
3	A Happy Time	128
4	Tom Is Up to Tricks	137
5	An Exciting Idea	152
6	Midnight Feast!	163
7	A Shock for the Feasters	172
8	A Shock for Tom – and One for Hugh	182
9	Things Are Cleared Up!	193
10	End of Term	203

CHAPTER 1

A NEW SCHOOL

'I don't want to go to boarding-school,' said Michael.

'Neither do I,' said Janet. 'I don't see why we have to, Mother!'

'You are very lucky to be able to go,' said Mother. 'Especially together! Daddy and I have chosen a mixed school for you – one with boys and girls together, so that both you and Mike can go together, and not be parted. We know how fond you are of one another. It's quite time you went too. I run after you too much. You must learn to stand on your own feet.'

Mother went out of the room. The two children stared at one another. 'Well, that's that,' said Janet, flipping a pellet of paper at Michael. 'We've got to go. But I vote we make our new school sit up a bit!'

'I've heard that you have to work rather hard

at St Rollo's,' said Mike. 'Well, I'm not going to! I'm going to have a good time. I hope we're in the same class.'

There was only a year between the two of them, and as Janet was a clever child, she had so far always been in the same form as her brother, who was a year older. They had been to a mixed school ever since they had first started, and although they now had to go away to boarding-school, they both felt glad that they were not to be parted, as most brothers and sisters had to be.

The last week of the holidays flew past. Mother took the children to the shops to get them fitted for new clothes.

'We do seem to have to get a lot for our new school,' said Janet, with interest. 'And are we going to have tuck-boxes, Mother, to take back with us?'

'If you're good!' said Mother, with a laugh.

Mother did get them their tuck-boxes — one each for them. She put exactly the same in each box — one big currant cake, one big ginger cake, twelve chocolate buns, a tin of toffee and a large bar of chocolate. The children were delighted.

The day came for them to go to their new school. They couldn't help feeling a bit excited, though they felt rather nervous too. Still, they were to go together, and that would be fun. They caught a train to London, and Mother took them to the station from which the school train was to start.

'St Rollo's School,' said the big blue label on the train. 'Reserved for St Rollo's School.' A great crowd of boys and girls were on the platform, talking and laughing, calling to each other. Some were new, and they looked rather lonely and shy. Janet and Mike kept together, looking eagerly at everyone.

'They look rather nice,' said Mike to Janet. 'I wonder which will be in our form.'

Both boys and girls were in grey, and looked neat and smart. One or two masters and mistresses bustled up and down, talking to parents, and warning the children to take their places. Janet and Mike got into a carriage with several other boys and girls.

'Hello!' said one, a cheeky-looking boy of about eleven. 'You're new, aren't you?'

'Yes,' said Mike.

'What's your name?' said the boy, his blue eyes twinkling at Mike and Janet.

'I'm Michael Fairley, and this is my sister Janet,' said Mike. 'What's your name?'

'I'm Tom Young,' said the boy. 'I should think you'll be in my form. We have fun. Can you make darts?'

'Paper darts,' said Mike. 'Of course! Everybody can!'

'Ah, but you should see my new kind,' said the boy, and he took out a note book with stiff paper leaves. But just as he was tearing out a sheet the guard blew his whistle, and the train gave a jerk.

'Goodbye, Mother!' yelled Mike and Janet. 'Goodbye. We'll write tomorrow!'

'Goodbye, my dears!' called Mother. 'Enjoy yourselves and work hard.'

The train left the station. Now that it was really gone the two children felt a bit lonely. It wasn't going to be very nice not to see Mother and Daddy for some time. Thank goodness they had each other!

Tom looked at them. 'Cheer up!' he said. 'I felt like that, too, the first time. But you soon get over it. Now just see how I make my new paper darts.'

Tom was certainly very clever with his fingers. In a minute or two he had produced a marvellous pointed dart out of paper, which, when it was thrown, flew straight to its mark.

'Better than most darts, don't you think?' said Tom proudly. 'I thought that one out last term. The first time I threw one it shot straight at Miss Thomas and landed underneath her collar. I got sent out of the room for that.'

Janet and Mike looked at Tom with much respect. All the other children in the carriage laughed.

'Tom's the worst boy in the school,' said a rosy-cheeked, fat girl. 'Don't take lessons from him – he just doesn't care about anything.'

'Is Miss Thomas a mistress?' asked Mike. 'Do we have masters *and* mistresses at St Rollo's?'

'Of course,' said Tom. 'If you're in my form you'll have Miss Thomas for class teacher, but a whole lot of other teachers for special subjects. I can tell you whose classes it's safe to play about in, and whose classes it's best to behave in.'

'Well, seeing that you don't behave well in *anybody's* classes, I shouldn't have thought you could have told anyone the difference,' said the fat girl.

'Be quiet, Marian,' said Tom. 'I'm doing the talking in this carriage!'

That was too much for the other children. They fell on Tom and began to pummel him. But he took it all good-humouredly, and pummelled back hard. Mike and Janet watched laughing. They didn't quite like to join in.

Everyone had sandwiches to eat. They could eat them any time after half-past twelve, but not before. Tom produced a watch after a while and looked at it.

'Good!' he said. 'It's half-past twelve.' He undid his packet of sandwiches. Marian looked astonished.

'Tom! It simply *can't* be half-past twelve yet,' she said. She looked at her wrist-watch. 'It's only a quarter-to.'

'Well, your watch must be wrong then,' said Tom, and he began to eat his sandwiches. Janet looked at her watch. It certainly was only a quarter-to-twelve. She felt sure that Tom had put his watch wrong on purpose.

It made the other children feel very hungry to watch Tom eating his ham sandwiches. They began to think it would be a good idea to put their watches fast, too! But just then a master came down the corridor that ran the length of the train. Tom tried to put away his packet of sandwiches, but he was too late.

'Well, Tom,' said the master, stopping at the door and looking in. 'Can't you wait to get to school before you begin to break the rules?'

'Mr Wills, sir, my watch says twenty-five-to-one,' said Tom, holding out his watch, with an innocent look on his face. 'Isn't it twenty-five-to-one?'

'You know quite well it isn't,' said Mr Wills. He took the watch and twisted the hands back. 'Put away your lunch and have it when your watch says half-past twelve,' he said. Tom gave a look at his watch. Then he looked up with an expression of horror.

'Sir! You've made my watch half an hour slow!

That would mean I couldn't start my lunch till one o'clock!'

'Well, well, fancy that!' said Mr Wills. 'I wonder which is the more annoying – to have a watch that is fast, or one that is slow, Tom? What a pity! You'll have to eat your lunch half an hour after the others have finished!'

He went out. Tom stared after him gloomily. 'I suppose he thinks that's funny,' he said.

Tom put away his lunch, for he knew quite well that Mr Wills might be along again at any moment. At half-past twelve all the other children took down their lunch packets and undid them eagerly, for they were hungry. Poor Tom had to sit and watch them eat. His watch only said twelve o'clock!

At one, when all the others had finished, he opened his lunch packet again. 'Now, of course,' he said, 'I'm so terribly hungry that ham sandwiches, egg sandwiches, buttered scones with jam, ginger cake, an apple and some chocolate won't nearly do for me!'

The train sped on. It was due to arrive at half-past two. When the time came near, Janet and Mike looked out of the windows eagerly. 'Can we see St Rollo's from the train?' asked Janet.

'Yes. It's built on a hill,' said Marian. 'You'll see it out of that window. It's of grey stone and it has towers at each end. In the middle of the

building is a big archway. Watch out for it now, you'll soon see it.'

The children looked out, and, as Marian had said, they caught sight of their new school. It looked grand!

There it stood on the hill with big towers at each end, built of grey stone. Creeper climbed over most of the walls, and here and there a touch of red showed that when autumn came the walls would glow red with the crimson leaves.

The train slowed down at a little station. Everyone got out. Some big coaches were waiting in the little station yard. Laughing and shouting, the children piled into them. Their luggage was to follow in a van. The masters and mistresses climbed in last of all, and the coaches set off to St Rollo's.

They rumbled up the hill and came to a stop before the big archway. The school looked enormous, now that the children were so close to it. All the boys and girls clambered down from the coaches and went in at a big door.

The two children followed Tom up the stairs to a large and cheerful room, into which the afternoon sun poured. A plump, smooth-cheeked woman was sitting there.

'Hello, Matron,' said Tom, going in. 'I've brought two new ones to see you. Are they in my dormitory? I hope they are.'

'Well, I'm sorry for them if they are!' said Matron, getting out a big exercise book and turning the pages. 'What are their names?'

'Michael and Janet Fairley,' said Mike.

Matron found their names and ticked them off.

'Yes – Michael is in your dormitory, Tom,' she said. 'Janet is across the passage with Marian and the girls. I hope they will help you to behave better, not worse. And just remember what I told you last term – if you play any tricks on me this term I'll send you to the headmaster!'

Tom grinned. He took Mike's arm and led him away with Janet. 'You'll soon begin to think I'm a bad lot!' he said. 'Come on – I'll show you everything.'

CHAPTER 2

SETTLING DOWN

There was plenty to see at St Rollo's. The dormitories were fine big rooms. Each child had a separate cubicle with white curtains to pull around their bed, their dressing-table, and small cupboard. The children's luggage was already in the dormitory when they got there.

'We'll unpack later,' said Tom. 'Look, that will be my bed. And yours can be next to mine, Mike, if I can arrange it. Look – let's pull your trunk into this cubicle, then no one else will take it.'

They pulled the trunk across. Then Tom showed Janet her dormitory, across the passage. It was exactly the same as the boys, except that the beds had pink eiderdowns instead of blue. After that, Tom showed them the classrooms, which were fine rooms, all with great windows looking out on the sunny playgrounds.

'This is our classroom, if you're in my form,' said Tom. Janet and Mike liked the look of it very much.

'I had that desk there at the front, last term,' said Tom, pointing to one. 'I always try to choose one right at the back – but sooner or later I'm always made to sit at the front. People seem to think they have to keep an eye on me. Awfully tiresome!'

'I wonder where our desks will be,' said Mike.

'Bag two, if you like,' said Tom. 'Just dump a few books in. Where do you want to sit?'

'I like being near the window, where I can look out,' said Mike. 'But I'd like to be where I can see you too, Tom!'

'Well, I shall try to bag a desk at the back as usual,' said Tom. He took a few books from a bookshelf and dumped them into a desk in the back row by the window. 'That can be your desk. That can be Janet's. And this can be mine! All in a row together.'

Tom showed them the playgrounds and the hockey fields. He showed them the marvellous gym and the assembly hall where the school met every morning for prayers. He showed them the changing-rooms, where they changed for games, and the common-rooms where each class met out of school to read, write or play games. Janet and Mike began to feel they would lose their way if they had to find any place by themselves!

'We'll go and unpack now,' said Tom. 'And then it'll be tea-time. Good! We can all have things out of our tuck-boxes today.'

They went to their dormitories to unpack. Janet parted from the two boys and went into hers. Marian was there, and she smiled at Janet.

'Hello,' she said. 'I saw Tom taking you round. He's a kind soul, but he'll lead you into trouble, if he can! Come and unpack. I'll show you where to put your things. I'm head of this dormitory.'

Janet unpacked and stowed away her things into the drawers of the dressing-table, and hung her coats in the cupboard. All the other girls were doing the same. Marian called to Janet.

'I say! Do you know any of the others here? That's Audrey near to you. And this is Bertha. And that shrimp is Connie. And here's Doris, who just simply can't help being top of the form, whether she tries or not!'

Doris laughed. She was a clever-looking girl, with large glasses on her nose. 'We're all in the same form,' she told Janet. 'Is your brother in Tom Young's dormitory?'

'Yes,' said Janet. 'Will he be in my form too?'

'Yes, he will,' said Doris. 'All the four dormitories on this floor belong to the same form. Miss Thomas is our form mistress. She's nice but pretty strict. Only one person ever gets the better of her – and that's Tom Young! He just simply doesn't care what he does – and he's always bottom. But he's nice.'

Meanwhile Mike was also getting to know the boys in his dormitory. Tom was telling him about them.

'See that fellow with the cross-eyes and hooked nose? Well, that's Eric.'

Mike looked round for somebody with cross-eyes and a hooked nose, but the boy that Tom pointed to had the straightest brown eyes and nose that Mike had ever seen! The boy grinned.

'I'm Eric,' he said. 'Don't take any notice of Tom. He thinks he's terribly funny.'

Tom took no notice. 'See that chap over there in the corner? The one with spots all over his face? That's Fred. He gets spots because he eats too many sweets.'

'Shut up!' said Fred. He had one small spot on his chin. He was a big, healthy-looking boy, with bright eyes and red cheeks.

'And this great giant of a chap is George,' said Tom, pointing to an under-grown boy with small shoulders. The boy grinned.

'You must have your joke, mustn't you?' he said amiably. 'And now Mike what-ever-your-name-is, let me introduce you to the world's greatest clown, the world's greatest idiot, Master

Thomas Henry William Young, biggest duffer and dunce, and, by a great effort, the bottom of the form!'

Mike roared with laughter. Tom took it all in good part. He gave George a punch which the boy dodged cleverly.

There was one other boy in the room, but Tom said nothing about him. He was not a pleasant-looking boy. Mike wondered why Tom didn't tell him his name. So he asked for it.

'Who's he?' he said, nodding his head towards the boy, who was unpacking his things with rather a sullen face.

'That's Hugh,' said Tom, but he said no more.

Hugh looked up. 'Go on, say what you like about me,' he said. 'The new boy will soon know it, anyway! Be funny at my expense if you want to!'

'I don't want to,' said Tom.

'Well, *I'll* tell him then,' said the boy. 'I'm a cheat! I cheated in the exams last term, and everyone knows it because Tom found it out and gave me away!'

'I didn't give you away,' said Tom. 'I've told you that before. I saw that you were cheating, and said nothing. But Miss Thomas found it out herself. Anyway, let's drop the subject of cheating this term. Cheat all you like. I don't care!'

Tom turned his back on Hugh. Mike felt very

awkward. He wished he hadn't asked for the boy's name. Eric began to talk about the summer holidays and all he had done. Soon the others joined in, and when Hugh slipped out of the room no one saw him go.

'It should be about tea-time now,' said Tom, pulling out his watch. 'Golly, no it isn't! Half an hour to go still! My word, what a swizz!'

Just then the tea-bell rang loudly, and Tom looked astonished. Mike laughed. 'Don't you remember?' he said. 'Mr Wills put your watch back half an hour?'

'So he did!' said Tom, looking relieved. He altered his watch again. 'Well, come on,' he said. 'I could eat a mountain if only it was made of cake! Bring your tuck-box. What have you got in it? I'll share mine with you if you'll share yours with me. I've got a simply *gorgeous* choco-late cake.'

It was fun, that first meal. All the children had brought goodies back in their tuck-boxes. They shared with one another, and the most enormous teas were eaten that day! Janet went to sit with Mike, and the two of them gave away part of all their cakes. In exchange they got slices of all kinds of other cakes. By the time they got up from the tea-table they couldn't eat another crumb!

'I hope we don't have to have supper!' said

Mike. 'I feel as if I don't want to eat again for a fortnight. But wasn't it scrumptious!'

The children had to go and see the headmaster and headmistress after tea. Both were grey-haired, and had kindly but rather stern faces. Mike and Janet felt very nervous and could hardly answer the questions they were asked.

'You will both be in the same form at first,' said the headmaster, Mr Quentin. 'Janet is a year younger, but I hear that she is advanced for her age. You will be in the second form.'

'Yes, sir,' said the children.

'We work hard at St Rollo's,' said Miss Lesley, the headmistress. 'But we play hard too. So you should have a good time and enjoy every day of the term. Remember our motto always, won't you: "Not the least that we dare, but the most that we can!"'

'Yes, we will,' said the two children.

'St Rollo's does all it can for its children,' said Miss Lesley, 'so it's up to you to do all you can for your school, too. You may go.'

The children went. 'I like the heads, don't you, Mike?' said Janet. 'But I'm a bit afraid of them too. I shouldn't like to be sent to them for punishment.'

'I bet Tom has!' said Mike. 'Now we've got to go and see Miss Thomas. Come on.'

Miss Thomas was in their classroom, making

out lists. She looked up as the two children came in.

'Well, Michael; well, Janet!' she said, with a smile. 'Finding your way round a bit? It's difficult at first, isn't it? I've got your last reports here, and they are quite good. I hope you will do as well for me as you seem to have done for your last form mistress!'

'We'll try,' said the children, liking Miss Thomas's broad smile and brown eyes.

'I'm bad at maths,' said Janet.

'And my handwriting is pretty awful,' said Michael.

'Well, we'll see what we can do about it,' said Miss Thomas. 'Now you can go back to the common-room with the others. You'll know it by the perfectly terrible noise that comes out of the door!'

The children laughed and went out of the room. 'I think I'm going to like St Rollo's very much,' said Janet happily. 'Everybody is so nice. The girls in my dorm are fine, Mike. Do you like the boys in yours?'

'Yes, all except a boy called Hugh,' said Mike, and he told Janet about the sulky boy. 'I say – is this our common-room, do you think?'

They had come to an open door, out of which came a medley of noises. A record player was going, and someone was singing loudly to it, rather out of tune. Two or three others were shouting about something and another boy was hammering on the floor, though why, Janet and Mike couldn't imagine. They put their heads in at the door.

'This can't be our common-room,' said Mike. 'The children all look too big.'

'Get out of here, tiddlers!' yelled the boy who was hammering on the floor. 'You don't belong here! Find the kindergarten!'

'What cheek!' said Janet indignantly, as they withdrew their heads and walked off down the passage. 'Tiddlers, indeed!'

Round the next passage was a noise that was positively deafening. It came from a big room on the left. A radio was going full-tilt, and a record player, too, so that neither of them could be heard properly. Four or five children seemed to be having a fight on the floor, and a few others were yelling to them, telling them to 'Go it!' and 'Stick it!'

A cushion flew through the air and hit Janet on the shoulder. She threw it back. A girl raised her voice dolefully.

'Oh, do shut up! I want to hear the radio!'

Nobody took any notice. The girl shouted even more loudly: 'I say, I WANT TO HEAR THE RADIO.'

Somebody snapped off the record player, and

the radio seemed to boom out even more loudly. There was dance music on it.

'Let's dance!' cried Fred, fox-trotting by, holding a cushion as if it were a partner. 'Hello, Mike, hello Janet. Where on earth have you been? Come into our quiet, peaceful room, won't you? Don't stand at the door looking like two scared mice.'

So into their common-room went the two children, at first quite scared of all the noise around them. But gradually they got used to it, and picked out the voices of the boys and girls they knew, talking, shouting, and laughing together. It was fun. It felt good to be there all together like a big, happy family. The noise was nice too.

For an hour the noise went on, and then died down as the children became tired. Books were got out, and puzzles. The radio was turned down a little. The supper-bell went, and the children trooped down into the dining-hall. The first day was nearly over. A quiet hour after supper, and then bed. Yes – it was going to be nice at St Rollo's!

CHAPTER 3
A HAPPY TIME

Michael and Janet found things rather strange at first, but after two or three days St Rollo's began to seem quite familiar to them. They knew their way about by then – though poor Janet got quite lost the second day, looking for her classroom!

She opened the door of what she thought was her form-room – only to find a class of big boys and girls taking painting! They sat round the room with their drawing-boards in front of them, earnestly drawing or painting a vase of bright leaves.

'Hello! What do you want?' asked the drawing-master.

'I wanted the second form classroom,' said Janet, blushing red.

'Oh well, this isn't it,' said the master. 'Go down the stairs, turn to the right – and it's the first door.'

'Thank you,' said Janet, thinking how silly she was not to remember what floor her classroom was on. She ran down the stairs, and tried to remember if the drawing-master had said turn to the left or to the right.

'I think he said left,' said Janet to herself. So to the left she turned and opened the first door there. To her horror, it was the door of the junior mistresses' common-room! One or two of them sat there, making out timetables.

'What is it?' said the nearest one.

'Nothing,' said Janet, going red again. 'I'm looking for my classroom – the second form. I keep going into the wrong room.'

'Oh, you're a new girl, aren't you?' said the mistress, with a laugh. 'Well, go along the passage and take the first door on the right.'

So at last Janet found her classroom, and was very relieved. But when three or four days had gone by she couldn't imagine how she could have made such a mistake! The school building, big as it was, was beginning to be very familiar to her.

The second form settled down well. Janet and Mike were the only new children in it. Miss Thomas let them keep the desks they had chosen – but she looked with a doubtful eye on Tom, when he sat down at the desk in the back row, next to Janet.

'Oh,' she said, 'so you've chosen a desk in the back row again, Tom. Do you think it's worth while doing that? You know quite well that before a week has gone by you will be told to take a desk out here in front, where I can keep my eye on you.'

'Oh, Miss Thomas!' said Tom. 'I'm turning over a new leaf this term. Really I am. Let me keep this desk. I'm trying to help the new children, so I'm sitting by them.'

'I see,' said Miss Thomas, who looked as if she didn't believe a word that Tom said. 'Well – I give you not more than a week there, Tom! We'll just see!'

There were a good many children in Mike's form. Mike and Janet soon got to know them all. They were a jolly lot, cheerful and full of fun – except for the boy called Hugh, who hardly spoke to anyone and seemed very sullen.

Tom was a great favourite. He made the silliest jokes, played countless tricks, and yet was always ready to help anyone. The teachers liked him, though they were forever scolding him for his careless work.

'It isn't necessary for you to be bottom of *every* subject, *every* week, is it, Tom?' said Miss Thomas. 'I mean – wouldn't you like to give me a nice surprise and be top in something just for once?'

'Oh, Miss Thomas – would it really give you a nice surprise?' said Tom. 'Wouldn't it give you a shock, not a surprise! I wouldn't like to give you a shock.'

Considering that you spend half your time thinking out tricks to shock people, that's a foolish remark!' said Miss Thomas. 'Now, open your books at page 19.'

Janet and Mike found the work to be about the same as they had been used to. They both had brains, and it was not difficult for them to keep up with the others. In fact, Janet felt sure that, if she tried very hard, she could be top of the form! She had a wonderful memory, and couldn't seem to forget anything she had read or heard. This was a great gift, for it made all lessons easy for her.

Doris, the girl with glasses, was easily top each week. Nothing seemed difficult to her. Even the hot-tempered French master beamed on Doris and praised her – though he seldom praised anyone else. Mike and Janet were quite scared of him.

'Monsieur Crozier looked as if he was going to shout at me this morning!' said Janet to Mike. 'Don't you think he did!'

'He will shout at you if you give him the slightest chance!' said Tom, with a grin. 'He shouted at me so loudly last term that I almost jumped out of my skin. I just got back into it in time.'

'Idiot!' said Mike. 'I bet you had played some sort of trick on him.'

'He had,' said Fred. 'He put white paint on that front lock of his hair – and when Monsieur Crozier exclaimed about it, what do you suppose Tom said?'

'What?' said Janet and Mike together.

'He said, "Monsieur Crozier, my hair is turning white with the effort of learning the French verbs you have given us this week",' said Fred. 'And do you wonder he got shouted at after that?'

'I'll think out something to make old Monsieur sit up!' said Tom. 'You wait and see!'

'Oh, hurry up, then,' begged the children around.

A week or two passed by, and Mike and Janet settled down well. They loved everything. The work was not too difficult for them. The teachers were jolly. Hockey was marvellous. This was played three times a week, and everyone was expected to turn up. Gym was fine too. Mike and Janet were good at this, and enjoyed the half-hours in the big gym with the others.

There were lovely walks around the school. The children were allowed to go for walks by themselves, providing that three or more of them went together. So it was natural that Tom, Mike and Janet should often go together. The other children made up threes too, and went off for an hour or so when they could. It was lovely on the hills around, and already the children were looking for ripe blackberries and peering at the nut trees to see if there were going to be many nuts.

'Doesn't Hugh ever go for a walk?' said Janet once, when she, Mike and Tom had come in from a lovely sunny walk, to find Hugh bent double over a book in a far corner of the common-room. He was alone. All the other children were out doing something – either practising hockey on the field, or gardening, or walking.

'Well, you have to be at least three to go for a walk,' said Tom in a low voice. 'And no one ever asks Hugh, of course – and he wouldn't like to ask two others because he'd be pretty certain they'd say no.'

'Why does everyone dislike him so?' asked Janet. 'He would be quite a nice-looking boy if only he didn't look so surly.'

'He was new last term,' said Tom. 'He's not very clever, but he's an awful swot – mugs up all sorts of things, and always has his nose in a book. Won't join in things, you know. And when he cheated at the exams last term, that was the last straw. Nobody decent wanted to have anything to do with him.'

'He can't be very happy,' said Janet, who was a kind-hearted girl, willing to be friends with anyone.

'Perhaps he doesn't deserve to be,' said Tom.

'But even if you don't deserve to be happy, it must be horrid never to be,' argued Janet.

'Oh, don't start being a ministering angel, Janet,' said Mike impatiently. 'Don't you remember how sorry you were for that spiteful dog next door, who was always being told off for chasing hens? Well, what happened when you went out of your way to be kind to him, because you thought he must be miserable? He snapped at you, and nearly took your finger off!'

'I know,' said Janet. 'But that was only because he couldn't understand anyone being kind to him.'

'Well, Hugh would certainly snap your head off if you tried any kind words on *him*,' said Tom, with a laugh. 'Look out – here he comes.'

The children fell silent as Hugh got up from his seat and made his way to the door. He had to pass the three on his way, and he looked at them sneeringly.

'Talking about me, I suppose?' he said. 'Funny how everyone stops talking when I come near!'

He bumped rudely into Janet as he passed and sent her against the wall. The two boys leapt at Hugh, but he was gone before they could hold him.

'Well, do you feel like going after him and being sweet?' said Tom to Janet. She shook her head. She thought Hugh was horrid. But all the same she was sorry for him.

Mike and Janet wrote long letters to their mother and father. 'We're awfully glad we came to St Rollo's,' wrote Mike. 'It's such fun to be with boys and girls together, and as Janet is in my form, we are as much together as ever we were. I shouldn't be surprised if she's top one week. The hockey is lovely. I'm good at it. Do send us some chocolate, if you can.'

His mother and father smiled at his letters and Janet's. They could see that the two children were happy at the school they had chosen for them and they were glad.

'St Rollo's is fine,' wrote Janet. 'I *am* glad we came here. We do have fun!'

They certainly did – and they meant to have even more fun very soon!

CHAPTER 4

TOM IS UP TO TRICKS

Tom was always up to tricks. He knew all the usual ones, of course – the trick of covering a bit of paper with ink one side, and handing it to someone as if it were a note – and then, when they took it they found their fingers all inky! He knew all the different ways of making paper darts. He knew how to flip a pellet of paper from underneath his desk so that it would land exactly where he wanted it. There was nothing that Tom didn't know, when it came to tricks!

He lasted just four days in his desk at the back. Then Miss Thomas put him well in the front!

'I thought you wouldn't last a week at the back there,' she said. 'I feel much more comfortable with you just under my eye! Ah – that's better. Now I think you will find it quite difficult to fire off your paper pellets at children who are really trying to work.'

The trick that had made Miss Thomas move him had caused the class a good deal of merriment. Miss Thomas had written history questions on the board for the form to answer in writing. Janet was hard at work answering them, for she wanted to get good marks, and Mike was working well too.

Suddenly Janet felt a nudge. She looked up. Tom had already finished answering the questions, though Janet felt certain that he had put 'I don't know' to some of them! Tom nodded his head towards the window.

Janet looked there. Just outside was one of the gardeners, hard at work in a bed. He was a large man, red-faced, with a very big nose.

'What about giving old Nosey a shock?' said Tom, opening his desk to speak behind it. Janet nodded gleefully. She didn't know what Tom meant to do, but she was sure it would be funny.

Tom hunted in his desk till he found what he wanted. It was a piece of clay. The boy shut his desk and warmed the clay in his hands below it. It soon became soft and he picked off pieces to make hard pellets.

Janet and Mike watched him. Miss Thomas looked up. 'Janet! Michael! Tom! Have you all finished your history questions? Then get out your textbook and learn the list of answers on page 23.'

The children got out their books. Tom winked at Janet. He waited until Miss Thomas was standing at Fred's desk, with her back turned to him, and then, very deftly, he flicked the clay pellet out of the open window with his thumb.

It hit the gardener on the top of his hat. He thought something had fallen on him from above and he stood up, raising his head to the sky, as if he thought it must be raining. Janet gave a muffled giggle.

'Shut up,' whispered Tom. He waited till the man had bent down again, and his big nose presented a fine target. Flick! A big pellet flew straight out of the window – and this time it hit the astonished man right on the tip of his nose, with a smart tap.

He stood up straight, rubbing his nose, glaring into the window. But all he saw were bent heads and innocent faces, though one little girl was certainly smiling very broadly to herself. That was Janet, of course. She simply could *not* keep her mouth from smiling!

The gardener muttered something to himself, glared at the bent heads, and bent over his work again. Tom waited for his chance and neatly flicked out another pellet. It hit the man smartly on the cheek, and he gave a cry of pain.

All the children looked up. Miss Thomas gazed in surprise at the open window, outside which the gardener was standing.

'Now, look here!' said the angry man, staring in at the window. 'Which of you did that? Hitting me in the face with peas or something! Where's your teacher?'

'I'm here,' said Miss Thomas. 'What is the matter? I don't think any of the children here have been playing tricks. You must have made a mistake. Please don't disturb the class.'

'Made a mistake! Do you suppose I don't know when anyone is flicking peas or something at me?' said the gardener. He glared at Janet, who was giggling. 'Yes – and that's the girl who did it, too, if you ask *me*! She was giggling to herself before – and I'm pretty certain I saw her doing it.'

'That will do,' said Miss Thomas. 'I will deal with the matter myself. I am sorry you have been hindered in your work.'

She shut down the window. The man went off, grumbling. Miss Thomas looked at Janet, who was very red.

'Kindly leave the gardeners to do their work, Janet,' she said in a cold voice. 'Bring your things out of your desk, and put them in the empty front one. You had better sit there, I think.'

Janet didn't know what to say. She couldn't give Tom away, and if she said she hadn't done it, Miss Thomas would ask who did, and then Tom would get into trouble. So with a lip that quivered, Janet opened her desk and began to get out her things.

Tom spoke up at once. 'It wasn't Janet,' he said. 'I did it. I didn't like the look of the gardener's nose – so I just hit it with a clay pellet or two, Miss Thomas. I'm sure you would have liked to do it yourself, Miss Thomas, if you had seen that big nose out there.'

Everyone choked with laughter. Miss Thomas didn't even smile. She looked straight at Tom with cold eyes.

'I hope my manners are better than yours,' she said. 'If not, I don't know what I should feel inclined to do to you, Tom Young. Bring your things out here, please. You will be under my eye in future.'

So, with many soft groans, Tom left his seat at the back beside Janet, and went to the front.

'Oh, what a pity,' said Janet, later on, as the class was waiting for Monsieur Crozier to come. 'Now you won't be able to do any more tricks, Tom. You're right at the front.'

'Goodness, you don't think that will stop Tom, do you?' said Fred. And Fred was right. It didn't!

Monsieur Crozier was not a very good person to play about with, because he had such a hot temper. The class never knew how he was going to take a joke. Sometimes, if Tom or Marian said something sharp, he would throw back his grey head and roar with laughter. Yet at other times he could not see a joke at all, but would fly into a temper.

Few people dared to play tricks on the French master, but Tom, of course, didn't care what he did. One morning, Janet and Mike found him kneeling down in a far corner of the room, behind the teacher's desk. In this corner stood two or three rolled-up maps. Tom was hiding something behind the maps.

'Whatever are you doing?' asked Janet in surprise. Tom grinned.

'Preparing a little surprise packet for dear Monsieur Crozier,' he said.

'What is it?' said Mike, peering down.

'Quite simple,' said Tom. 'Look – I've got two empty cotton-reels here – and I've tied thin black thread to each. If you follow the thread you'll see it runs behind this cupboard – behind that bookcase, over the hot-water pipe, and up to my desk. Now, what will happen when I pull the threads?'

'The cotton-reels will dance in their corner!' giggled Janet, 'and Monsieur Crozier won't know what the noise is – because over here is far from where anyone sits! What fun!'

Mike told everyone what was going to happen. It was a small trick but might be very funny. The whole class was thrilled. In the French lesson that day they were to recite their French verbs, which was a very dull thing to do. Now it looked as if the lesson wouldn't be dull after all.

Monsieur Crozier came into the room, his spectacles on his nose. His thick hair was untidy. It was plain that he had been in a temper with somebody, for it was his habit to ruffle his hair whenever he was angry. It stood up well, and the class smiled to see it.

'*Asseyez-vous!*' rapped out Monsieur Crozier, and the class sat down at once. In clear French sentences the master told them what he expected of them. Each child was to stand in turn and recite the French verb he had been told to learn, and the others were to write them out.

'And this morning I expect HARD WORK!' said the French master. 'I have had disgraceful work from the third form – disgrrrrrrrrraceful! I will not put up with the same thing from you. You understand?'

'Yes, Monsieur Crozier,' chanted the class. Monsieur Crozier looked at Tom, who had on a most innocent expression that morning.

'And you, too, will work!' he said. 'It is not necessary always to be bottom. If you had no brains I would say "Ah, the poor boy – he cannot work!" But you have brains and you will not use them. That is bad, very bad.'

'Yes, sir,' said Tom. Monsieur Crozier gave a grunt and sat down. Fred stood up to recite his verbs. The rest of the class bent over their desks to write them.

They were all listening for Tom to begin his trick. He did nothing at first, but waited until Fred had sat down. There was silence for a moment, whilst the French master marked Fred's name in his book.

Then Tom pulled at the threads which ran to his desk. At once the cotton-reels over in the far corner began to jiggle like mad. Jiggle, jiggle, jiggle! they went. Jiggle, jiggle, jiggle!

Monsieur Crozier looked up, puzzled. He didn't quite know where the noise came from. He stared round the quiet class. Everyone's head was bent low, for most of the children were trying to hide their smiles. Janet felt a giggle coming and she shut her mouth hard. She was a terrible giggler. Mike looked at her anxiously. Janet so often gave the game away by exploding into a tremendous laugh.

The noise stopped. Doris stood up to say her verbs. She was quite perfect in them. She sat down. Monsieur Crozier marked her name. Tom pulled at the threads and the cotton reels jerked madly about behind the maps.

'What is that noise?' said the master impatiently, looking round. 'Who makes that noise?'

'What noise, sir?' asked Tom innocently. 'Is there a noise? I heard an aeroplane pass over just now.'

'An aeroplane does not make a noise in this room!' said the master. 'It is a jiggling noise. Who is doing it?'

'A jiggling noise, sir?' said Mike, looking surprised. 'What sort of jiggling noise? My desk is a bit wobbly, sir – perhaps it's that you heard?'

Mike wobbled his desk and made a terrific noise. Everyone laughed.

'Enough!' cried Monsieur Crozier, rapidly losing his temper. 'It is not your desk I mean. Silence! We will listen for the noise together.'

There was a dead silence. Tom did not pull the threads. There was no noise at all.

But as soon as Eric was standing up, reciting his verbs in his soft voice, Tom jerked hard at his threads, and the reels did a kind of foxtrot behind the maps, sounding quite loud on the boards.

'There is that noise again!' said the master angrily. 'Silence, Eric. Listen!'

Tom could not resist making the reels dance again as everyone listened. Jiggle-jiggle-jiggle-tap-tap-tap-jiggle-jiggle they went, and the class began to giggle.

'It comes from behind those maps,' said the French master, puzzled. 'It is very strange.'

'Mice perhaps, sir,' said Mike. Tom flashed him a grin. Mike was playing well.

The French master did not like mice. He stared at the maps, annoyed. He did not see how the noise could possibly be a trick, for the maps were far from any child's desk.

'Shall I see, sir?' asked Tom, getting up. 'I don't mind mice a bit. I think Mike may be right, sir. It certainly does sound like a mouse caught behind there. Shall I look, sir?'

Now, what Tom thought he would do was to look behind the maps, pocket the reels quickly after pulling the threads away, and then announce that there was no mouse there. But when he got to the corner, he couldn't resist carrying the trick a bit further.

'I'll pretend there really *is* a mouse!' he thought. 'That'll give the class a real bit of fun!'

So, when he knelt down and fiddled about behind the maps, pulling away the threads and getting hold of the cotton-reels, he suddenly gave a yell that made everyone jump, even the French master.

'It's a mouse! It's a mouse! Come here, you bad little thing! Sir, it's a mouse!'

The class knew perfectly well it wasn't. Janet gave a loud, explosive giggle that she tried hastily to turn into a cough. Even the surly Hugh smiled.

Tom knocked over all the maps, pretending to get the mouse. Then he made it seem as if the little creature had run into the classroom, and he jumped and bounded after the imaginary mouse, crawling under desks and nearly pulling a small table on top of him. The whole class exploded into a gale of laughter that drowned Monsieur Crozier's angry voice.

'Come here, you!' yelled Tom, thoroughly enjoying himself. 'Ah – got you! No, I haven't! Just touched your tail. Ah, there you are again. Whoops! Nearly got you that time. What a mouse! Oh, what a mouse! Whoops, there you go again!'

Mike got out of his desk to join him. The two boys capered about on hands and knees and nearly drove Monsieur Crozier mad. He hammered on his desk. But it was quite impossible for the class to be silent. They laughed till their sides ached.

And in the middle of it all Miss Thomas walked in, furious! She had been taking the class next door, and could not imagine what all the noise was. She had felt certain that no teacher was with the second form. She stopped in

surprise when she saw Monsieur Crozier there, red in the face with fury.

The class stopped giggling when they saw Miss Thomas. She had a way of giving out rather unpleasant punishments, and the class somehow felt that she could not readily believe in their mouse.

'I'm sorry, Monsieur Crozier,' said Miss Thomas. 'I thought you couldn't be here.'

'Miss Thomas, I dislike your class,' said Monsieur Crozier, quite as ready to fly into a temper with Miss Thomas as with the children. 'They are ill-disciplined, ill-behaved, ill-mannered. See how they chase a mouse round your classroom! Ah, the bad children!'

'A mouse!' said Miss Thomas, in the utmost surprise. 'But how could that be? There are no mice in the school. The school cats see to that. Has anyone got a tame mouse then?'

'No, Miss Thomas,' chorused the children together.

'We heard a noise behind the maps,' began Tom – but Miss Thomas silenced him with a look.

'Oh, you did, did you?' she said. 'You may as well know that I don't believe in your mouse, Tom. I will speak to you all at the beginning of the next lesson. Pardon me for coming in like this, Monsieur Crozier. I apologise also for my class.'

The class felt a little subdued. The French master glared at them, and proceeded to give them so much homework that they would have groaned if they had dared. Tom got shouted at when he opened his mouth to protest. After that, he said no more. Monsieur Crozier was dangerous when he got as far as shouting!

Miss Thomas was very sarcastic about the whole affair when she next saw her class. She flatly refused to believe in the mouse, but instead, asked who had gone to examine the noise in the corner.

'I did,' said Tom, who always owned up to anything, quite fearlessly.

'I thought so,' said Miss Thomas. 'Well, you will write me an essay, four pages long, on the habits of mice, Tom. Give it to me this evening.'

'But Miss Thomas,' began Tom, 'you know it's the hockey match this afternoon, and we're all watching it, and after tea there's a concert.'

'That doesn't interest me at all,' said Miss Thomas. 'What interests me intensely at the moment is the habits of mice, and that being so, I insist on having that essay by seven o'clock. Not another word, Tom, unless you also want to write me an essay on, let us say, cotton-reels. I am not quite so innocent as Monsieur Crozier.'

After that there was no more to be said. Mike and Janet gave up watching the hockey match in order to help Tom with his essay. Mike looked up the habits of mice, and Janet looked up the spelling of the words. With many groans and sighs Tom managed to write four pages in his largest handwriting by seven o'clock. 'It *is* decent of you to help,' he said gratefully.

'Well, we shared the fun, didn't we?' said Mike. 'So we must share the punishment too!'

CHAPTER 5

AN EXCITING IDEA

In the middle of that term Mike's birthday came. He was very much looking forward to it because he knew he would have plenty of presents sent to him, and he hoped his mother would let him have a fine birthday cake.

'I hope it won't be broken in pieces before it arrives,' he said to Janet. 'You know, Fred had a birthday last term, and he said his cake came in crumbs, and they had to eat it with a spoon. I'd better warn Mother to pack it very carefully.'

But Mother didn't risk packing one. She wrote to Mike and told him to order himself a cake from the big cake shop in the town nearby. 'And if you would like to give a small party to your own special friends, do so,' she said. 'You can order what you like in the way of food and drink, and tell the shop to send me the bill. I can trust you not to be too extravagant, I know.

Have a good time, and be sure your birthday cake has lots of icing on.'

Mike was delighted. He showed the letter to Tom. 'Isn't Mother decent!' he said. 'Can you come down to the town with Janet and me to-day, Tom, and help me to order things?'

'You're not going to ask all the boys and girls in the class to share your party, are you?' said Tom. 'You know, that would cost your mother a small fortune.'

'Would it?' said Mike. 'Well – what shall I do, then? How shall I choose people without making the ones left out feel hurt?'

'Well, if I were you, I'd just ask the boys in your own dormitory, and the girls in Janet's,' said Tom. 'That will be quite enough children.'

'Yes, that's a good idea,' said Mike, pleased. 'I wish we could have our party in a separate room, so that the others we haven't asked won't have to see us eating the birthday cake and the other things. That would make me feel rather mean.'

'Well, listen,' said Tom, looking excited. 'Why not have a midnight feast? We haven't had one for two terms. It's about time we did.'

'A midnight feast!' said Janet, her eyes nearly popping out of her head. 'Oooh, that would be marvellous. I've read about them in books. Oh Mike, *do* let's have your party in the middle of the night. Do, do!'

Mike didn't need much pressing. He was just as keen on the idea as Janet and Tom! The three of them began to talk excitedly about what they would do.

'Shall we have it in one of our dormitories?' said Janet. 'Either yours or mine, Mike?'

'No,' said Tom at once. 'Mr Wills sleeps in the room next to ours – and Miss Thomas sleeps in the room next to yours, Janet. Either of them might hear us making a noise and come and find us.'

'We needn't make a noise,' said Janet. 'We could just eat and drink.'

'Janet! You couldn't possibly last an hour or two without going off into one of your giggling fits, you know you couldn't,' said Mike. 'And you make an awful noise with your first giggle. it's like an explosion.'

'I know,' said Janet. 'I can't help it. I smother it till I almost burst – and then it comes out all of a sudden. Well – if we don't have the feast in one of our dormitories, where *shall* we have it?'

They all thought hard. Then Tom gave a grin. 'I know the very place. What about the gardeners' shed?'

'The gardeners' shed!' said Mike and Janet together. 'But why there?'

'Well, because it's out of the school and we can make a noise,' said Tom. 'And because it's not far from the little side-door we use when we go to the playing-fields. We can easily slip down and open it to go out. And also, it would be a fine place to store the food in. We can put it into boxes and cover them with sacks.'

'Yes – it does sound rather good,' said Mike. 'It would be marvellous to be out of the school building, because I'm sure we'd make a noise.'

'Last time we had a midnight feast, we had it in a dormitory,' said Tom. 'And in the middle someone dropped a ginger-beer bottle. We got so frightened at the noise that we all hopped into bed, and the feast was spoilt. If we hold ours in the shed, we shan't be afraid of anyone coming. Let's!'

So it was decided to hold it there. Then the next excitement was going down to the town to buy the food.

They went to the big cake shop first. Mike said what he wanted. 'I want a big birthday cake made,' he said. 'Enough for about twelve people, please. And I want it to be covered with pink icing, and written on it in white I'd like *A happy birthday*. Can you do that?'

'Certainly,' said the shopgirl, and wrote down Mike's name, and his mother's address, so that she might send her the bill. Then Mike turned to the others. 'What else shall we have?' he said. 'You help me to choose.'

So Janet and Tom obligingly helped him, and between them they chose chocolate cakes, biscuits, shortbread and currant buns. Then they went to the grocer and asked for tinned sweetened milk, which everyone loved, sardines, tinned pineapple, and bottles of ginger-beer.

The shop promised to pack up the goods and have them ready for the children to collect on the morning of Mike's birthday. The children meant to go down immediately after morning school and fetch the things.

They felt very excited. Janet and Mike counted up the cakes and things they had ordered and felt sure they had bought enough to feed everyone very well indeed.

'And now we'll have to ask everyone,' said Mike happily. 'Isn't it fun to invite people, Janet?'

'I'll ask the girls in my dorm tonight,' said Janet. 'The rest of the class won't be there then, so they won't know. I vote we don't tell anyone except our guests that we're going to have a feast. We don't want it to get to the ears of any of the teachers. Tell the boys in your dorm to keep it quiet, Mike.'

'Right,' said Mike. Then he frowned. 'I say, Janet,' he said, 'what about Hugh? Are we to ask him?'

Janet stared at Mike. She didn't know what to

say. 'Well, I suppose we'd better,' she said at last. 'It would be rather awful to leave him out as he belongs to your dormitory. No one likes him – but still he'd feel simply awful if he knew we were having a feast and he hadn't been asked.'

'All right,' said Mike. 'I'll ask him. But he's such a surly fellow that he'll be an awful wet blanket.'

Tom agreed that Hugh must be asked too. 'I don't want him,' he said, 'but, after all, he belongs to our dorm, and it would make him feel pretty dreadful to be left out when everyone else is going.'

So Mike quite meant to ask Hugh too. But then, something happened to make him change his mind. It had to do with Tom, and it happened in Mr Wills's class.

Mr Wills was taking maths with the second form. Tom was bored. He hated maths, and seldom got a sum right. Mr Wills had almost given him up. So long as Tom sat quietly at his desk and didn't disturb the others, Mr Wills left him in peace. But if Tom got up to any tricks Mr Wills pounced on him.

Tom usually behaved himself in the maths class, for he respected Mr Wills, and knew that he would stand no nonsense. But that morning he was restless. He had slept very well the night before and was so full of beans that he could hardly sit still. He had prepared a trick for the French master in the next lesson, and was longing to play it.

The trick was one of his string tricks. He was marvellous at those. He had slipped into the classroom before school that morning and had neatly tied strong yellow thread to the pegs that held the blackboard on its easel. A jerk at the thread, and a peg would come out – and down would crash the blackboard!

Tom looked at Mr Wills. Mr Wills caught his eye and frowned. 'Get on, Tom,' he said. 'Don't slack so. If you can't get a sum right, get it wrong. Then, at least, I shall know you've been doing something!'

'Yes, Mr Wills,' said Tom meekly. He scribbled down a few figures that meant nothing at all. His hand itched to pull away the peg. As his desk was at the front, he could easily leap forward and pick up the peg before Mr Wills could see that string was tied to it.

'It's a bit dangerous to try it on with Mr Wills,' thought Tom. 'But I'm so bored I must do something!'

He turned round and caught Mike's eye. Mike winked. Tom winked back, then he winked twice with each eye in turn. That was his signal to Mike that a trick was about to be played! Mike nudged Janet. They both looked up

eagerly. Hugh caught their eager looks and wondered what was up. He guessed that Tom was
about to play a trick and he watched him.

Mr Wills was at the back of the room, looking
at Bertha's work. Tom jerked his thread. The peg
of the easel flew out – one side of the blackboard
slipped down – and then it fell with a resound-
ing crash on to the floor, making everyone jump
violently. Mike and Janet knew what had happened, and they tried not to laugh. Hugh also
saw what had happened. Before anyone could do
anything Tom was out of his desk in a flash, and
had picked up the blackboard and peg and set
them back in place. He wondered whether or not
to remove the threads, but decided he would risk
it again.

'Thank you, Tom,' said Mr Wills, who hadn't
for a moment guessed that it was a trick. 'Get on
with your work, everybody.'

Most of the children guessed that it was Tom
up to his tricks again. They watched to see if it
would happen once more. Mr Wills went to see
Hugh's work. He had done most of his sums
wrong, and the master grumbled at him.

'You haven't been trying! What have you been
thinking of to put down this sum like that! No
one else in the class has so many sums wrong!'

Hugh flushed. He always hated being grumbled at in front of anyone. 'I'm sure Tom has

more sums wrong than I have,' he said, in a low voice.

At that moment Tom jerked the two pegs neatly out of the easel, and the board fell suddenly, with an even greater crash than before. Everyone giggled, and Janet gave one of her explosions. The noise she made caused the children to laugh even more loudly.

'What's the matter with the board this morning?' said Mr Wills irritably.

'I should think Tom has something to do with it,' said Hugh spitefully. 'You'll find he hasn't got a single sum right – and has given all his attention to our blackboard instead. I have at least been working!'

There was a silence. Mr Wills went to the blackboard. He examined the pegs. But they now had no thread on them, for Tom had slipped it off and it was safely in his pockets.

But not very safely, after all! Mr Wills turned to Tom. 'Just turn out your pockets, please,' he ordered. Tom obeyed promptly – and there on the desk lay the tell-tale yellow thread, still with the little slip-knots at one end.

'I'll see you after the class, Tom,' said Mr Wills. 'I can't make you do good work – but I can at least stop you from preventing the others from working. You should know by now that I don't stand any nonsense in my classes.'

'Yes, sir,' said Tom dolefully.

'Maths is a most important subject,' went on Mr Wills. 'Some of the children here are working for scholarships and it is necessary they should get on well this term. If you disturb my classes once more I shall refuse to have you in them.'

'Yes, sir,' said Tom again, going red. Mr Wills had a very rough tongue. When the master had turned his back on the class to write something on the now steady blackboard, Tom turned round to get the comfort of a look from Mike and Janet. They nodded at him – and then Tom caught sight of Hugh's face.

Hugh wore a spiteful grin on his face. He was pleased to have got Tom into trouble.

'Sneak!' whispered Mike to Hugh.

'SILENCE!' said Mr Wills, not turning round. Mike said no more, but gave Hugh a look that said all his tongue longed to say!

'Wait till after school!' said the look. 'Just wait till after school.'

CHAPTER 6

MIDNIGHT FEAST!

Tom got a tremendous scolding after the class, and entered the French class four minutes late, with a very red face. Monsieur Crozier looked at him in surprise.

'And why are you late?' he said. 'It is not the custom to walk into my classes after they have started.'

'Please, sir, I'm sorry,' said Tom, 'but Mr Wills was talking to me.'

The French master guessed that Tom had been up for a scolding, and he said no more. Tom was very subdued that lesson. Mr Wills had said some cutting things to him, and the boy felt rather ashamed of himself. It was all very well to play tricks and have a good time – but there *was* work to do as well! So he sat like a lamb in the French class, and really listened to the lesson.

After school, Mike, Janet and Fred went after

Hugh. 'Sneak!' said Mike furiously. 'What did you want to go and give Tom away for?'

'Why shouldn't I?' said Hugh. 'He sneaked on me last term.'

'No, he didn't,' said Mike. 'He says he didn't – and you know as well as anybody that Tom's truthful. He doesn't tell lies. You're a beastly sneak!'

'Oh, shut up,' said Hugh rudely, and walked off. But the others walked after him, telling him all kinds of truthful but horrid things about himself. Hugh went into a music room to practise and banged the door on them. He even turned the key in the lock.

'He really is a spiteful sneak,' said Janet. 'Mike, you're surely not going to ask him to our feast now, are you?'

'You bet I'm not,' said Mike. 'As if I'd have a sneaky creature like that on my birthday night! No fear!'

'Well, we'll ask all the others, and we'll warn them not to say a word to Hugh,' said Janet. So they asked everyone else – Fred, Eric, small George, Marian, Bertha, Connie, Audrey and Doris. With Mike, Janet and Tom there would be eleven children altogether.

'And don't say a single word to anyone outside our dormitories,' said Mike. 'And don't say anything to Hugh, either. He's such a sneak that I'm not asking him. I'm sure if he got to know we were having a feast he'd prowl round and then tell about it! So, not a word, mind!'

Mike's birthday came. He had a lot of cards and many presents. A good deal of it was money and he meant to spend it in the holidays. His mother and father sent him a new paintbox and pencil-box with his name on them. His grandfather wrote to say that he had bought him a new bicycle. Janet gave him a box of writing paper and stamps. The others gave him small presents, pencils, rubbers, sweets, and so on. Mike was very happy.

'After school, we'll pop down with baskets and get all those things,' he said. 'We'd better ask one or two of the others to come too. We'll never be able to carry all the stuff ourselves.'

So Fred and Marian came too, and the five set off with giggles and talk. They came back with all the food and drink, and undid the birthday cake in the gardeners' shed. It was simply marvellous.

A *happy birthday* was written across it, and the pink icing was thick and not too hard. It was a fine big cake. The children were delighted. Mike put it carefully back into its box.

The gardeners' shed was a big place. It was piled with boxes, tools, pots, wood and so on. Actually it was not much used, for the gardeners had another, smaller shed they preferred, and they used the big shed mostly as a storehouse. The children soon found a good hiding-place for their food and drink.

There was an enormous old case, made of wood, at the back of the shed. They put everything into this and then put a board on top. On the board they piled rows of flower pots.

'There,' said Mike. 'I don't think anyone would guess what is under those pots! Now, let's arrange what we're going to sit on.'

There were plenty of boxes and big flower pots. The children pulled them out and arranged them to sit on. 'We shall have to pin sacks across the windows,' said Mike. 'Else the light of our candles will be seen.'

'Better do that this evening,' said Tom. 'It might make people suspicious if they came by and saw sacks across the windows.'

So they left the windows uncurtained. There was nothing else they could do except smuggle in a few mugs and plates and spoons. Janet said she could do this with Marian. She knew where the school crockery was kept, and she could easily slip into the big cupboard after handwork that afternoon and get what was needed. They could wash it after the feast and put it back again.

'I think that's everything,' said Mike happily.

'I say – this is going to be fun, isn't it! Golly, I can hardly wait till tonight!'

'I'll wake the girls in my dorm,' said Janet, 'and you wake the boys, Mike. Don't wake Hugh by mistake, though!'

Everything went off as planned. Janet fell asleep, but awoke just before midnight. She switched on her torch and looked at her watch. Five minutes to twelve! She slipped out of bed, put on shoes, stockings, vest, under her night-dress, and jersey over it. Then her dressing-gown on top. She woke the other girls one by one, shaking them and whispering into their ears.

'It's time! Wake up! The midnight feast is about to begin!'

The girls awoke, and sat up, thrilled. They began to put on vests and jerseys too. Meanwhile the boys were doing the same thing. Mike had awoken them all, except, of course, Hugh, and in silence they were dressing. They did not dare to whisper, as the girls could, because they were afraid of waking Hugh.

They all crept out of the dormitory, and found the six girls waiting for them in the passage out-side. Janet was trying to stop her giggles.

'For goodness' sake don't do one of your explo-sions till we're out in the shed,' said Mike anx-iously. So Janet bit her lips together and waited. They all went down the stairs and out of the little side-door. Then across to the big shed. Mike opened the door and everyone filed in. Once the door was shut, the children felt safe and began to talk in loud whispers.

Mike and Tom quickly put sacks across the three windows, and then lit three candles. Their wavering light made peculiar shadows in the shed, and everything looked rather mysterious and exciting. The other children watched Mike and Tom go to the box at the back and lift off the flowerpots arranged there.

And then out came the good things to eat and drink! How the children gaped for joy to see them! They all felt terribly hungry, and were pleased to see so much to eat and drink.

Mike set the birthday cake down on a big box. All the children crowded round to look at it. They thought it was marvellous. 'We'll cut it the very last thing,' said Mike. 'And don't forget to wish, everybody, because it's a birthday cake!'

They made a start on sardines and cake. It was a lovely mixture. Then they went on to currant buns and biscuits, pineapple and tinned milk. They chattered in low voices and giggled to their hearts' content. When Fred fell off his box and upset tinned, sticky milk all over himself, there was a gale of laughter. Fred looked so funny with his legs in the air, and milk dripping all over him!

'Sh! Sh!' said Mike. 'Honestly, we'll wake up the whole school! Shut up, Janet! Your giggles make everyone worse still. You just make me want to giggle myself.'

'This is the best feast we've ever had,' said Tom, helping himself to a large piece of chocolate cake. 'Any more ginger-pop, Mike?'

'Yes,' said Mike. 'Help yourself – and now, what about cutting the grand birthday cake?'

'It looks big enough for the whole school,' giggled Marian. 'I say – I wish Hugh knew what he was missing! Wouldn't he be wild! I expect he is still sound asleep in his bed.'

But Hugh wasn't! He had awakened at about half-past twelve, and had turned over to go to sleep again.

And then something strange had struck him. There was something missing in the dormitory. It was quite dark there and the boy could see nothing. But he lay there, half-asleep, wondering what was missing.

Then suddenly he knew. There was no steady breathing to be heard. There was no sound at all. Hugh sat up, alarmed. Why was nobody breathing? That was the usual sound to be heard at night, if anyone woke up. What had happened?

Hugh switched on his torch and got out of bed. He looked round the curtains that separated his cubicle from the next boy's. The bed was empty!

Hugh looked at all the beds. Every one was empty. Then the boy guessed in a flash what was happening.

'It's Mike's birthday – and he's having a midnight party somewhere. The beast! He's asked everyone else, and not me! I bet Janet's dormitory is empty too.'

He slipped out to see. It was as he had guessed – quite empty. All the beds were bare, their coverings turned back. The boy felt angry and hurt. They might have asked him! It was hateful to be left out like this.

'I'm always left out of everything!' he thought, hot tears pricking his eyelids. 'Always! Do they think it will make me behave any better to them if they treat me like this! How I hate them! I'll jolly well spoil their feast for them. That will serve them right!'

CHAPTER 7

A SHOCK FOR
THE FEASTERS

Hugh wondered how to spoil the feast.
Should he go and knock on Mr Wills's
door and tell him that the dormitories were
empty? No – Mr Wills didn't look too kindly on
tale-bearing. Well, then, he had better find out
where the children were feasting and spoil it for
them.

He looked out of the window, and by a chance
he caught sight of a tiny flicker outside. It came
from a corner of the big window of the shed. The
sack didn't quite cover the glass. Hugh stood
and looked at it, wondering where the light
came from.

'It's from the big shed,' he thought. 'So that's
where they're feasting. I'll go down and find
out!'

Down he went, out of the door, which the
children had left open, and into the yard. He

went across to the shed, and at once heard the sounds of laughter and whispering inside. He put his eye to the place in the window where the light showed, and saw the scene inside. It was a very merry one.

Empty bottles of ginger-beer lay around. Empty tins stood here and there, and crumbs were all over the place. It was plain that the two dormitories had had a marvellous time. Hugh's heart burned in him. He felt so angry and so miserable that he could almost have gone into the shed and fought every child there!

But he didn't do that. He knew it would be no use. Instead, he took up a large stone and crashed it on to the window! The glass broke at once, with a very loud noise. All the children inside the shed jumped up in fright, their cake falling from their fingers.

'What's that?' said Mike in a panic. 'The window is broken. Who did it?'

There was another crash as the second window broke under Hugh's stone. The children were now really afraid. They simply couldn't imagine what was happening.

'The noise will wake everyone up!' cried Mike, in a loud whisper. 'Quick, we'd better get back to our dormitories. Leave everything. There isn't time to clear up.'

Hugh didn't wait to break the third window.

He had seen a light spring up in Mr Wills's room above and he knew the master would be out to see what was happening before another minute had gone by. So he sped lightly up the stairs, and was in his bed before the door of Mr Wills's room opened.

The eleven children opened the door of the shed and fled into the school. They went up the stairs and into the passage where their dormitories were – and just as they were passing Mr Wills's door it opened! Mr Wills stood there in his dressing-gown, staring in amazement at the procession of white-faced children slipping by.

'What are you doing?' he asked. 'What was all that noise?'

The children didn't wait to answer. They fled into their rooms and hopped into bed, half-dressed as they were, shoes and all. Mr Wills went into the boys' dormitory, switched on the light and looked sternly round. He pulled back the curtains from those cubicles that had them drawn around, and spoke angrily.

'What is the meaning of this? Where have you been? Answer me!'

Nobody answered. The boys were really frightened. Hugh's bed was nearest to Mr Wills, and the master took hold of Hugh's shoulder, shaking him upright.

'You, boy! Answer me! What have you been doing?'

'Sir, I've been in bed all the evening,' said Hugh truthfully. 'I don't know what the others have been doing. I wasn't with them.'

Mr Wills glared round at the other beds. 'I can see that you are half-dressed,' he said in an icy voice. 'Get out and undress and then get back into bed. I shall want an explanation of this in the morning. You can tell the girls when you see them, that I shall want them too. It seems to me that this is something the Heads should know about. Now then – quick – out of bed and undress!'

The boys, all but Hugh, got out of bed and took off their jerseys and other things. Mr Wills told Hugh to get out of bed too.

'But I'm not half-dressed,' said Hugh. 'I've only got my pyjamas on, sir. I wasn't with the others.'

But Mr Wills wasn't believing anyone at all that night. He made Hugh get out too, and saw that he was in his pyjamas as he said. He did not notice one thing – and that was that Hugh had his shoes on! But Mike noticed it.

He was puzzled. Why should Hugh have his shoes on in bed? That was a funny thing to do, surely. And then the boy suddenly guessed the reason.

'Hugh woke up – saw the beds were empty – put on his shoes and slipped down to find us. It was he who broke the windows, the beast! He's got us all into this trouble!'

But he said nothing then. He would tell the others in the morning. He slipped back into bed and tried to go to sleep.

All the eleven children were worried when the morning came. They couldn't imagine what Mr Wills was going to do. They soon found out. Mr Wills had gone to the two Heads, and it was they that the children were to see, not Mr Wills. This was worse than ever!

'You will go now,' said Mr Wills, after prayers were over. 'I don't want to hear any explanations from you. You can tell those to the Heads. But I may as well tell you that I went down into the shed last night and found the remains of your feast, the candles burning – and the windows smashed. I understand the feast part – but why you should smash the windows is beyond me. I am ashamed of you all.'

'We didn't smash . . .' began Mike. But Mr Wills wouldn't listen to a word. He waved them all away. Hugh had to go, too, although he kept saying that he hadn't been with the others. Mike had told the others what he suspected about Hugh, and every boy and girl looked at him with disgust and dislike.

They went to see the Heads. Their knees shook, and Bertha began to cry. Even Janet felt the tears coming. All the children were tired, and some of them had eaten too much and didn't feel well.

The Heads looked stern. They asked a few questions, and then made Tom tell the whole story.

'I can understand your wanting to have some sort of a party on Michael's birthday,' said Miss Lesley, 'but to end it by smashing windows is disgusting behaviour. It shows a great lack of self-control.'

'I think it was Hugh who broke the windows,' said Mike, not able to keep it back any longer. 'We wouldn't have done that, Miss Lesley. For one thing we would have been afraid of being caught if we did that — it made such a noise. But, you see, we left Hugh out of the party — and I think that out of spite he smashed the windows to give us a shock, and to make sure we would be caught.'

'Did you do that, Hugh?' asked the headmaster, looking at the red-faced boy.

'No, sir,' said Hugh, in a low voice. 'I was in bed asleep. I don't know anything about it.'

'Well, then, why was it you had your shoes on in bed when Mr Wills made you get out last night?' burst out Tom. 'Mike saw them!'

Hugh said nothing, but looked obstinate. He

meant to stick to his story, no matter what was said.

The punishment was very just. 'As you have missed almost a night's sleep, you will all go to bed an hour earlier for a week,' said Miss Lesley.

'And you will please pay for the mending of the windows,' said the headmaster. 'You too, Hugh. I am not going to go into the matter of how the windows got broken – but I think Michael is speaking the truth when he says that he would not have thought of smashing windows because of the noise. All the same, you will all twelve of you share for the mending of the windows. I will deduct it from your pocket-money.'

'And please remember, children, that although it is good to have fun, you are sent here to work and to learn things that will help you to earn your living later on,' said Miss Lesley. 'There are some of you here working for scholarships, and you will not be able to win them if you behave like this.'

The children went out, feeling very miserable. It was hateful to go to bed early – earlier even than the first-formers. And they felt bitter about the payment for the windows, because they themselves had not broken them.

'Though if we hadn't held the feast, the windows wouldn't have been broken,' said Mike. 'So in a way it was because of us they got smashed.

But I know it was Hugh who did it, out of spite. Let's not say a word to him. Let's send him to Coventry and be as beastly as we can.'

So Hugh had a very bad time. He was snubbed by the whole of his class. The first and third-formers joined in too, and nobody ever spoke a word to him, unless it was a whispered, 'Sneak! Tell-Tale! Sneak!' which made him feel worse than if he had not been spoken to.

He worried very much over the whole thing. It was awful to have no friends, terrible to be treated as if he were a snake. He knew it was stupid and wrong to have broken the windows like that. He had done it in a fit of spiteful temper, and now it couldn't be undone.

He couldn't sleep at night. He rose the next day looking white and tired. He couldn't do his work, and the teachers scolded him, for he was one of the children who were going in for the scholarship. He couldn't remember what he had learnt, and although he spent hours doing his prep, he got poor marks for it.

Hugh knew that he must win the scholarship, for his parents were not well-off and needed help with his schooling. He had brothers and a sister who were very clever, and who had won many scholarships between them. Hugh didn't want to let his family down. He mustn't be the only one who couldn't do anything.

'The worst of it is, I haven't got good brains, as they have,' thought the boy, as he tried to learn a list of history dates. 'Everything is hard to me. It's easy to them. Daddy and Mother don't realise that. They think I must be as clever as the rest of the family, and I'm not. So they get angry with me when I'm not top of my form, though, goodness knows, I swot hard enough and try to be.'

The children all paid between them for the windows. They were mended and the remains of the feast were cleared away. The week went by, and the period for early going to bed passed by too. The children began to forget about the feast and its unfortunate ending. But they didn't forget their dislike for Hugh.

'I shan't speak a word to him for the rest of the term,' said Fred. And the others said the same. Only Janet felt sorry for the boy, and noticed how white and miserable he looked. But she had to be loyal to the others, and so she said nothing to him too, and looked away whenever he came near.

'I can't stick this!' Hugh thought to himself. 'I simply can't. I wish I could run away! I wish I was old enough to join a ship and go to sea. I hate school!'

CHAPTER 8

A SHOCK FOR TOM – AND ONE FOR HUGH

The days slipped by, and each one was full of interest. Janet and Mike liked their work, and loved their play. They loved being friends with Tom, and they liked all the others in their form, except Hugh.

The great excitement now was handwork. The boys were doing carpentry, and the things they were making were really beginning to take shape. The girls were doing raffia-work and were weaving some really lovely baskets. Janet couldn't help gloating over the basket she was making. It was a big work-basket for her mother, in every bright colour Janet could use. Mike was making a very fine pipe-rack for his father.

But the finest thing of all that was being made in the carpentry class was Tom's. The boy was mad on ships, and he had made a beautiful model. He was now doing the rigging, and the slender masts were beginning to look very fine indeed, set with snowy sails and fine thread instead of ropes.

There were wide window-sills in the hand-work and carpentry room, and on these the children set out their work, so that any other form could see what they were doing. They all took a deep interest in what the others were making. Tom's ship was greatly admired and the boy was really very proud of it.

'I think this is the only class you really work in, Tom, isn't it?' the woodwork master said, bending over Tom's model. 'My word, if you worked half as hard in the other classes as you do in mine, you would certainly never be bottom. You're an intelligent boy – yes, very intelligent – and you can use your brains well when you want to.'

Tom flushed with pleasure. He gazed at his beautiful shop and his heart swelled with pride as he thought of how it would look on his mantelpiece at home, when it was quite finished. It was almost finished now – he was soon going to paint it. He hoped there would be time to begin the painting that afternoon.

But there wasn't. 'Put your things away,' said the master. 'Hurry, Fred. You mustn't be late for your next class.'

The children cleared up, and put their models

on the wide window-sills. The master opened the windows to let in fresh air, and then gave the order to file out to the children's own classroom, two floors below. The handwork rooms were at the top of the school, lovely big light rooms, with plenty of sun and air.

The next lesson was geography. Miss Thomas wanted a map that was not in the corner and told Hugh to go and get it from one of the cupboards on the top landing. The children stood up to answer questions whilst Hugh was gone.

In the middle of the questions, something curious happened. A whitish object suddenly fell quickly past the schoolroom windows and landed with a dull thud on the stone path by the bed. The children looked round in interest. What could it have been? Not a bird, surely?

Mike was next to the window. He peeped out to see what it was – and then he gave a cry of dismay.

'What's the matter?' asked the teacher, startled.

'Oh, Miss Thomas – it looks as if Tom's lovely ship is lying broken on the path outside,' said Mike. Tom darted to the window. He gave a wail of dismay.

'It *is* my ship! Somebody has pushed it off the window-sill, and it's smashed. All the rigging is spoilt! The masts are broken!'

The boy's voice trembled, for he had really loved his ship. He had spent so many hours making it. It had been very nearly perfect.

There was a silence in the room. Everyone was shocked, and felt very sorry for Tom. In the middle of the silence the door opened and Hugh came in, carrying the map.

At once the same thought flashed into everyone's mind. Hugh had been to the top of the school to get the map – the cupboard was opposite the woodwork room – and Hugh had slipped in and pushed Tom's ship out of the window to smash it!

'You did it!' shouted Mike. Hugh looked astonished.

'Did what?' he asked.

'Smashed Tom's ship!' cried half a dozen voices.

'I don't know what you're talking about,' said Hugh, really puzzled.

'That will do,' said Miss Thomas. 'Tom, go and collect your ship. It may not be so badly damaged as you think. Hugh, sit down. Do you know anything about the ship?'

'Not a thing,' said Hugh. 'The door of the woodwork room was shut when I went to get the map.'

'Story-teller!' whispered half a dozen children.

'Silence!' rapped out Miss Thomas. She was

worried. She knew that Tom had been hated by Hugh ever since last term, and she feared that the boy really had smashed up the ship. She made up her mind to find out about it from Hugh himself, after the lesson. She felt sure she would know if the boy were telling her the truth or not, once she really began to question him.

But it was not Miss Thomas that Hugh feared. It was the children! As soon as morning school was over they surrounded him and accused him bitterly, calling him every name they could think of.

'I didn't do it, I didn't do it,' said Hugh, pushing away the hands that held him. 'Don't

pin everything on to me simply because I have done one or two mean things. I didn't do that. *I* liked Tom's ship, too.'

But nobody believed him. They gave the boy a very bad time and by the time that six o'clock came, Hugh was so battered by the children's looks and tongues that he crept up to his dormitory to be by himself. Then the tears came and he sobbed to himself, ashamed because he could not stop.

'I'm going away,' he said. 'I can't stay here now. I'm going home. Daddy and Mother will be angry with me, but I won't come back here. I can't do anything right. I didn't smash that lovely ship. I liked it just as much as the others did.'

He began to stuff some of his clothes into a small case. He hardly knew what he was doing. He knew there was a train at a quarter to seven. He would catch that.

The other children wondered where he was. 'Good thing for him he's not here,' said Fred. 'I've thought of a few more names to call him, the horrid beast!'

They were all in their common-room, discussing the affair. Tom's ship stood on the mantelpiece, looking very sorry for itself. The woodwork master came to see it.

'It's not as bad as it might be,' he said cheerfully. 'Just a bit dented here. Those masts can easily be renewed, and you can do the rigging again. You're good at that. Cheer up, Tom!'

The master went out. 'All very well for him to talk like that,' said Tom gloomily. 'But it isn't his ship. I don't feel the same about it now it's spoilt.'

There came a knock at the common-room door. It was such a timid, faint knock that at first none of the children heard it. Then it came again, a little louder.

'There's someone knocking at the door,' said Audrey, in astonishment, for no one ever knocked at their door.

'Come in!' yelled the whole form. The door opened and a first-former looked in. It was a small boy, with a very white, scared face.

'Hello, Pete, what's up!' said Fred.

'I w-w-w-want to speak to T-t-t-tom,' stammered the small boy, whose knees were knocking together in fright.

'Well, here I am,' said Tom. 'Don't look so scared. I shan't eat you!'

The small boy opened and shut his mouth like a fish, but not another word came out. The children began to giggle.

'Peter, whatever's the matter?' cried Janet. 'Has somebody frightened you?'

'N-n-n-no,' stammered Pete. 'I want to tell Tom something. But I'm afraid to.'

'What is it?' asked Tom kindly. He was always kind to the younger ones, and they all liked him. 'What have you been doing? Breaking windows or something?'

'No, Tom — m-m-m-much worse than that,' said the boy, looking at Tom with big, scared eyes. 'It's — it's about your lovely ship. That ship there,' and he pointed to the mantelpiece.

'Well, what about it?' said Tom, thinking that Pete was going to tell him how he had seen Hugh push it out of the window.

'Oh, Tom, it was my fault it got broken!' wailed the little boy, breaking into loud sobs. 'I was in the woodwork room with Dick Dennison, and we were fooling about. And I fell against the window-sill — and — and —'

'Go on,' said Tom.

'I put out my hand to save myself,' sobbed Pete, 'and it struck your lovely ship — and sent it toppling out of the open window. I was so frightened, Tom.'

There was a long silence after this speech. So Hugh hadn't anything to do with the ship, after all! No wonder he had denied it so vigorously. All the children stared at the white-faced Pete.

'I d-d-d-didn't dare to tell anyone,' went on the small boy. 'Dick swore he wouldn't tell either. But then we heard that you had accused Hugh of doing it — and we knew we couldn't do anything but come and own up. So I came because it was me that pushed it out – quite by accident, Tom.'

'I see,' said Tom slowly. He looked at the scared boy and gave him a kindly push. 'All right. Don't worry. You did right to come and tell me. Come straight away another time you do anything, old son – you see, we've done an injustice to somebody else – and that's not good. Go along back to your common-room. I daresay I can manage to mend the ship all right.'

The small boy gave Tom a grateful look out of tearful eyes, and shot out of the room at top speed. He tore back to his common-room, feeling as if a great load had been taken off his heart.

When he had gone, the children looked at one another. 'Well, it wasn't Hugh after all,' said Janet, saying what everyone else was thinking.

'No,' said Tom. 'It wasn't. And I called him a good many beastly names. For once they were unjust. And I hate injustice.'

Everyone felt uncomfortable. 'Well, anyway, he's done things just as horrid,' said Fred. 'It's no wonder we thought it was him. Especially as he just happened to be by the woodwork room at the time.'

'Yes,' said Mike. 'That was unlucky for him. What are we going to do about it?'

Nobody said anything. Nobody wanted to

apologise to Hugh. Tom stared out of the window.

'We've got to do something,' he said. 'Where is he? We'd better find him and get him here, and then tell him we made a mistake. We were ready enough to be beastly – now we must be ready to be sorry.'

'I'll go and find him,' said Janet. She had remembered Hugh's startled face as the others had suddenly accused him when he had come into the room carrying the map. She thought, too, of his miserable look when they had all pressed round him after tea, calling him horrid names. They had been unjust. Hugh had done many mean things – but not that one. Janet suddenly wanted to say she was sorry.

She sped into the classroom. Hugh wasn't there. She ran to the gym. He wasn't there either. She looked into each music room, and in the library, where Hugh often went to choose books. But he was nowhere to be found.

'Where can he be?' thought the little girl. 'He can't be out. His clothes are hanging up. What has he done with himself?'

She thought of the dormitory. She ran up the stairs, and met Hugh just coming out, carrying a bag, with the marks of tears still on his face. She ran up to him.

'Hugh! Where have you been? What are you

doing with that bag? Listen, we want you to come downstairs.'

'No, you don't,' said Hugh. 'None of you want me. I'm going home.'

'Hugh! What do you mean?' cried Janet, in alarm. 'Oh, Hugh, listen. We know who broke Tom's ship. It was little Pete. He pushed it out of the window by accident! Don't go home, Hugh. Come down and hear what we have to say!'

CHAPTER 9

THINGS ARE CLEARED UP!

But Hugh pushed past Janet roughly. He did not mean to change his mind. Janet was scared. It seemed a dreadful thing to her that Hugh should run away because of the unkindness he had received from his class. She caught hold of the boy and tried to pull him back into the dormitory.

'Don't,' said Hugh. 'Let me go. You're just as bad as the others, Janet. It's no good your trying to stop me now.'

'Oh, do listen to me, Hugh,' said Janet. 'Just listen for half a minute. Pete came and owned up about the ship. He pushed it out of the window when he was fooling about. And now you can't think how sorry we are that we accused you.'

Hugh went back into the dormitory, and sat on the bed. 'Well,' he said bitterly, 'you may feel pretty awful about it — but just think how I must feel always to have you thinking horrid things about me, and calling me names, and turning away when you meet me. And think how I felt when I woke up the other night and found everyone had gone to a midnight feast – except me! *You've* never been left out of anything. Everyone likes you. You don't know what it's like to be miserable.'

Janet took Hugh's cold hand. She was very troubled. 'Hugh,' she said, 'we did mean to ask you to our feast. Mike and Tom and I planned that we would. We didn't want you to be left out.'

'Well, why didn't you ask me then?' demanded Hugh. 'It would have made all the difference in the world to me if only you had. I'd have felt terribly happy. As it was you made me lose my temper and do something horrid and spiteful. I've been ashamed of it ever since. I spoilt your feast – and got you all into trouble. I wanted to do that, I know – but all the same I've been ashamed. And now that I'm going to run away, I want you to tell the others something for me.'

'What?' asked Janet, almost in tears.

'Tell them I *did* break the windows, of course,' said Hugh, 'and tell them that I want to pay for them. They had to pay a share – well, give them this money and let them share it out between them. I wanted to do that before, only I kept saying I hadn't broken the windows, so I couldn't very well offer to pay, could I? But now I can.'

Hugh got out his leather purse and took out some silver. He counted it and gave it to Janet. 'There you are,' he said. 'I can't do much to put right what I did, but I can at least do this. Now goodbye, Janet, I'm going.'

'No, don't go, Hugh, please don't,' said Janet, her voice trembling. 'Please come down and let us all tell you we're sorry. Don't go.'

But Hugh shook off her hand and went quickly down the stairs, carrying his little bag. Janet flew down the common-room, tears in her eyes and the money in her hand. She burst in at the door, and everyone turned to see what she had to say.

'I found him,' said Janet. 'He's – he's running away. Isn't it dreadful? He says he's ashamed of himself now for breaking the windows, and he's given me the money to give you, to pay for the whole amount. And oh Mike, oh Tom, somehow I can understand now why he broke those windows – he was so miserable at being left out!'

'I do wish we hadn't accused him unjustly,' began Fred. 'It's an awful pity he cheated last term like that. He seemed quite a decent chap till then – but somehow we got it into our heads after that that he was a dreadful boy and we didn't really give him a chance.'

'Look here – I'm going after him,' said Tom suddenly. 'If the Heads get to know about this, we'll all get into awful trouble, and goodness knows what will happen to Hugh. What's the time? Half-past six? I can catch him then, before he gets on the train.'

He ran out of the school building and went to the shed where Mr Wills's bicycle was kept. He wheeled it out and jumped on it. He didn't stop to light the lamp. Down the drive he went and out of the great school gates.

He pedalled fast, for it was quite a way to the station. He kept his eyes open for Hugh, but it was not until he had almost come to the station that he saw the boy. Hugh was running fast. He had been running all the way, because he had been so afraid of missing the train.

Tom rode up close to him, jumped off the bicycle, clutched Hugh's arm and pulled him to the side of the road. He threw the bicycle against the hedge, and then dragged the astonished boy into a nearby field.

'What's up? Oh, it's you, Tom! Let me go. I'm going home.'

'No, you're not,' said Tom. 'Not until you hear what I've got to say, anyway. Listen, Hugh. We're ashamed of ourselves. We really are. It's true you've been pretty beastly and spiteful – but it was partly because of us. I mean, we made you behave like that. I see that now. If we'd behaved differently you might have, too. You were a decent chap till the end of last term. We all liked you.'

'I know,' said Hugh, in a low voice. 'I was happy till then. Then I cheated. I know there's no excuse for cheating – but I had a reason for my cheating. It seemed a good reason to me then, but I see it wasn't now.

'Somehow or other I had to pass that exam,' said Hugh. 'All my brothers and my sister are clever and pass exams and win scholarships, and my father said I mustn't let the family down. I must pass mine too. Well, I'm not really clever. That is why I have to swot so hard, and never have time to play and go for walks as the rest of you do. So, as I was afraid I'd not pass the exam, I cheated a bit. And you gave me away.'

'I didn't,' said Tom. 'I saw you'd cheated, but I didn't give you away. Why don't you believe that? Miss Thomas found it out.'

'Do you swear you didn't give me away?' said Hugh.

'I swear I didn't!' said Tom. 'You've never known me to sneak, have you, or to tell lies? I do a lot of silly things and play the fool, but I don't do mean things.'

'All right. I believe you,' said Hugh. 'But I can't tell you how the thought of that cheating, and knowing that you all knew it, weighed on my mind. You see, I'm not really a cheat.'

'I see,' said Tom. 'It's really your parents' fault for trying to drive you too hard. You're silly. You should tell them.'

'I'm going to,' said Hugh. 'That's one thing I'm going home to say now. And I've been so miserable this term that what brains I have won't work at all! So it's no good me trying for the scholarship anyhow. Somehow things aren't fair. There's you with brains, and you don't bother to use them. There's clever Janet and Mike, and they fool about and don't really try to be top when they could. And there's me, with poor brains, doing my very best and getting nowhere.'

Tom suddenly felt terribly ashamed of all his fooling and playing. He felt ashamed of making Mike and Janet do bad work too, for they none of them really tried their hardest. He bit his lip and stared into the darkness.

'I've done as much wrong as you have,' he said at last. 'You cheated because you hadn't got good enough brains – and I've wasted my good brains and not used them. So I've cheated too, in another way. I never thought of it like that before. Hugh, come back with me. Let's start again. It's all been a stupid mistake. Look –

give us a chance to show you we're sorry, won't you?'

'You didn't give *me* a chance,' said Hugh.

'I know. So you can feel awfully generous if you will give *us* a chance!' said Tom. 'And look here, old son – I'm not going to waste my good brains any more and cheat the teachers out of what I could really do if I tried – I'm going to work hard. I'll help you, if you'll help me. I don't know how to work hard, but you can show me – and I'll help you with my brains. See?'

Just then a loud whistle came from the station and then a train pulled out. Hugh looked at the train.

'Well, the train's gone,' he said. 'So I can't go with it. I'll have to come back with you. Let me sleep over it and see how I feel in the morning. I don't want to see any of you again tonight. I should feel awkward. If I make up my mind I can begin all over again, I'll nod at you when we get up – and just let's all act as if nothing had happened. I can't stand any more of this sort of thing. I simply *must* work if I'm going to enter for that scholarship.'

The two boys went back together. Hugh went straight upstairs to his dormitory, telling Tom to say that he didn't want any supper. But before he went, Hugh held out his hand.

There was a warm handshake between the two

of them and then Tom went soberly back to the common-room, wondering what to say. The children crowded round him and Tom explained what had happened.

When they heard what Hugh had said about how he was expected to do as well as his brothers and sister, and how he knew he hadn't good enough brains, they were silent. They knew then why Hugh had swotted so much. They even understood why he had been tempted to cheat. Every child knew how horrid it was to disappoint parents or let their family down.

'Well, let's hope he'll make up his mind to stay,' said Tom. 'And listen – I feel quite a bit ashamed of *my* behaviour too. My parents pay for me to learn things here, and I never try at all – except in woodwork. I just fool about the whole time, and make you laugh. Well, from now on, I'm going to do a spot of work. And so are you, Mike and Janet. You've neither of you been top once this term, and you could easily be near it, and give Doris a shock!'

'All right,' said Janet, who had been thinking quite a lot too, that night. 'I'll work. Miss Thomas said today she would give me a bad report because I've not been doing my best. I don't want that. Mike will work too. We always do the same.'

Hugh was asleep when the children went up to bed. For the first night for a long time he was at peace, and slept calmly without worrying. Things had been cleared up. He was happier.

In the morning the boys got up when the bell went. Tom heard Hugh whistling softly to himself as he dressed, and he was glad. Then a head was put round Tom's curtains, and Tom saw Hugh's face. It was all smiles, and looked quite different from usual.

Tom stared at the smiling head. It nodded violently up and down and disappeared. Tom felt glad. Hugh was doing the sensible thing –

starting all over again, and giving the others a chance to do the same thing!

And what a change there was for Hugh that morning when the boys and girls met in their common-room! He was one of them now, not an outcast – and everyone felt much happier because of it.

CHAPTER 10
END OF TERM

Miss Thomas and the other teachers had a pleasant shock that week. For the first time since he had been at St Rollo's Tom began to work! The teachers simply couldn't understand it. Not only Tom worked, though – Mike and Janet did too.

'Something's happened that we don't know about,' said Miss Thomas to Mr Wills. 'And do you notice how much happier that boy Hugh looks? It seems as if the others have decided to be nicer to him. It's funny how Tom seems to have made friends with him all of a sudden. They even seem to be working together!'

So they were. They did their prep. together, and learnt many things from each other. Tom's quick brains were useful at understanding many things that Hugh's slow brains did not take in – and Hugh's ability for really getting down to things, once he understood them, was a fine example for the rather lazy Tom.

'You make a good team,' said Miss Thomas approvingly. 'I am pleased with you both. Tom, I think it would be a good idea to move you away from that front desk, and put you beside Hugh. You can help one another quite a lot.'

'Oooh, good,' said Tom, his eyes gleaming. 'It does rather cramp my style, Miss Thomas, to be under your eye all the time, you know.'

The class laughed. They had been surprised at Tom's sudden change of mind regarding his work. But they were afraid that he might no longer fool about as he used to do. He always caused so much amusement – it would be sad if he no longer thought of his amazing tricks.

'Don't worry,' said Tom, when Mike told him this. 'I shall break out at times. I can't stop thinking of tricks even if I'm using my brains for my work too!'

He kept his word, and played one or two laughable tricks on poor Monsieur Crozier, nearly driving him mad. Tom provided him with a pen on his desk, which on being pressed for writing, sent out a stream of water from its end. The French master was so angry that he threw the blackboard chalk down on the floor and stamped on it.

This thrilled the class immensely, and was

talked of for a long time. In fact, that term, on the whole, was a very exciting one indeed. Mike and Janet got quite a shock when they realised that holidays would begin in a week's time!

'Oh! Fancy the term being so nearly over!' said Janet dolefully.

'Gracious, Janet, don't you want to be home for Christmas?' said Marian.

'Yes, of course,' said Janet. 'But it's such fun being at St Rollo's. Think of the things that have happened this term!'

Miss Thomas overheard her. She smiled. 'Shall I tell you what is the most surprising thing that has happened?' she said.

'What?' asked the children, crowding round. Miss Thomas held the list of marks for the last week in her hand. She held it up.

'Well, for the first time this term Tom Young isn't bottom!' she said. 'I couldn't believe my eyes when I added up the marks – in fact I added them all up again to make sure. And it's true – he actually isn't bottom. Really, the world must be coming to an end!'

Everyone roared with laughter. Tom went red. He was pleased.

'I suppose I'm next to bottom, though,' he said, with a twinkle.

'Not even that!' said Miss Thomas. 'You are sixth from the top – simply amazing. And Hugh has gone up too – he is seventh. And as for Mike and Janet – well, wonders will never cease! They tie for second place, only two marks behind Doris!'

Mike, Janet, Tom and Hugh were delighted. It really was nice to find that good work so soon showed results. Hugh took Tom's arm.

'I can't tell you how you've helped me,' he said. 'Not only in my work – in other ways too. I feel quite different.'

The children thought that Hugh looked different too. He smiled and laughed and joked with the others, and went for walks as they did. Who would have thought that things could possibly have turned out like that, after all?

The term came quickly to an end. There were concerts and handwork exhibitions – and, not quite so pleasant, exams as well! All the children became excited at the thought of Christmas, pantomimes, presents and parties, and the teachers had to make allowances for very high spirits.

The last day came. There was a terrific noise everywhere, as packing went on in each dormitory, and boys and girls rushed up and down the stairs, looking for pencil-boxes, books, boots, shoes and other things. There were collisions everywhere, and squeals of laughter as things rolled down the stairs with a clatter.

'I suppose all this noise is necessary,' sighed

Mr Wills, stepping aside to avoid somebody's football, which was bouncing down the stairs all by itself, accompanied above by a gale of laughter. 'Dear me – how glad I shall be to say goodbye to all you hooligans! What a pity to think you are coming back next term!'

'Oh no, sir – we're glad!' shouted Mike, rushing down after the football. 'We shall love the holidays – but it will be grand to come back to St Rollo's!'

Goodbyes were said all round. Some of the children were going home by train, some by car.

'Good!' said Janet. 'We don't need to say goodbye till we get to London. Look – there's our coach at the door. Come on!'

They piled into the big coach, with about twenty other children. It set off to the station. The children looked back at the big grey building.

'Goodbye St Rollo's,' said Mike. 'See you next term. Goodbye! Goodbye!'

The Boy
Who Wanted a Dog

The Boy
Who Wanted a Dog

Enid Blyton
Illustrations by Gareth Floyd

BLOOMSBURY
CHILDREN'S
BOOKS

Contents

1	When Granny Came to Tea	219
2	All Because of a Kitten	225
3	A Job for Donald	231
4	Donald Goes to Work!	237
5	A Wonderful Evening	243
6	Sunday Afternoon	249
7	Donald is Very Busy	256
8	Donald Gets into Trouble	262
9	In the Middle of the Night	268
10	A Shock for Donald!	274
11	Good Old Prince!	280
12	Surprise for Donald	286
13	A Wonderful Day	292
14	Donald – and his Dog!	298

CHAPTER 1

WHEN GRANNY
CAME TO TEA

'Hello, Granny!' said Donald, rushing in from afternoon school. 'I hope you've come to tea!'

'Yes, I have!' said Granny. 'And I've come to ask you a question, too. It's your birthday soon – what would you like me to give you?'

'He really doesn't deserve a birthday present,' said his father, looking up from his paper. 'His weekly reports from school haven't been good.'

'Well, Dad – I'm not brainy like you,' said Donald, going red. 'I do try. I really do. But arithmetic beats me, I just *can't* do it. And I just hate trying to write essays and things – I can't seem to think of a thing to say!'

'You *can* work if you want to,' said his mother, beginning to pour out the tea. 'Look what your master said about your nature work – "Best work in the whole form. Knows more about birds and animals than anyone." Well, why can't you do well at writing and arithmetic!'

'They're not as interesting as nature,' said Donald. 'Now, when we have lessons about dogs and horses and squirrels and birds, I don't miss a word! And I write jolly good essays about *them*!'

'Did you get good marks today?' asked his father.

Donald shook his head, and his father frowned. 'I suppose you sat dreaming as usual!' he said.

'Well – geography was so dull this morning that I somehow couldn't keep my mind on it,' said Donald. 'It was all about things called peninsulas and isthmuses.'

'And what *were* you keeping your mind on – if it happened to be working?' asked his father.

'Well – I was thinking about a horse I saw when I was going to school this morning,' said Donald, honestly.

'But why think of a *horse* in your geography lesson?' said his mother.

'Well, Mother – it was a nice old horse, and doing its best to pull a heavy cart,' said Donald. 'And I couldn't help noticing that it had a dreadful sore place on its side, that was being rubbed by the harness. And oh, Mother, instead of being sorry for the horse, the man was hitting it!'

'And so you thought of the horse all through your geography lesson?' said Granny, gently.

'Well, I couldn't help it,' said Donald. 'I kept wondering if the man would put something on the sore place, when he got the horse home. I kept thinking what *I* would do if it were my horse. Granny, people who keep animals should be kind to them, and notice when they are ill or hurt, shouldn't they?'

'Of course they should,' said Granny. 'Well, don't worry about the horse any more. I'm sure the man has tended it by now. Let's talk of something happier. What would you like for your birthday?'

'Oh Granny – there's something I want more than anything else in the world!' said Donald, his eyes shining.

'Well, if it's not *too* expensive and is possible to get, you shall have it!' said Granny. 'What is it?'

'A puppy!' said Donald, in an excited voice. 'A puppy of my very own! I can make him a kennel myself. I'm good with my hands, you know!'

'*No*, Donald!' said his mother, at once. 'I will *not* have a dirty little puppy messing about the house, chewing the mats to pieces, rushing about tripping everyone up, and . . .'

'He wouldn't! He wouldn't!' said Donald. 'I'd train him well. He'd walk at my heels. He could sleep in my bedroom on a rug. He could . . .'

'Sleep in your room! Certainly not!' said his mother quite shocked. 'No, Granny – *not* a puppy, please. Donald's bad enough already, the things he brings home – caterpillars, a hedgehog – ugh, the prickly thing – a stray cat that smelt dreadful and stole the fish out of the larder – and . . .'

'Oh Mother – I wouldn't bring *any*thing into the house if only you'd let me have a puppy!' said Donald. 'It's the thing I want most in the world. A puppy of my very own! Granny, please, please give me one.'

'NO,' said his father. 'You don't *deserve* a puppy while your school work is so bad. Sorry, Granny. You'll have to give him something else.'

Granny looked sad. 'Well, Donald – I'll give you some books about animals,' she said. 'Perhaps your father will let you have a puppy when you get a fine school report.'

'I never will,' said poor Donald. 'I'm not nearly as clever as the other boys, except with my hands. I'm making you a little foot-stool, Granny, for *your* birthday. I'm carving a pattern all round it – and the woodwork master said that even *he* couldn't have done it better. I'm good with my hands.'

'You've something else that is good too,' said Granny. 'You've a good heart, Donald, and a kind one. Well, if you mayn't have a puppy for your birthday, you must come with me to the bookshop and choose some really lovely books. Would you like one about dogs – and another about horses, or cats?'

'Yes. I'd like those very much,' said Donald. 'But oh – how I'd *love* a puppy.'

'Let's change the subject,' said his father. 'What about tea? I see Mother has made some of her chocolate cakes for you, Granny. Donald, forget this puppy business, please, and take a chair to the table for Granny.'

So there they all are, sitting at the tea-table,

eating jam sandwiches, chocolate buns and biscuits. Donald isn't talking very much. He is thinking hard – 'dreaming', as his teacher would say.

'Where would I keep the puppy if I had one?' he thinks. 'Let me see – I could make a dear little kennel, and put it in my own bit of garden. How pleased the puppy would be to see me each morning. What should I call him – Buster? Scamper? Wags? Barker? No – he mustn't bark, Mother would be cross. I'll teach him to . . .'

'Look! Donald's dreaming again!' said his mother. 'Wake up, Donald! Pass Granny the buns! I wonder what you're dreaming about *now*!'

Granny knew! She smiled at him across the table. Dear Donald! *Why* couldn't she give him the puppy that he so much wanted?

CHAPTER 2

ALL BECAUSE OF A KITTEN

Two days later Donald had quite an adventure! It was all because of a kitten. He was walking home from school, swinging his satchel, and saying 'Hello' to all the dogs he met, when he suddenly saw a kitten run out of a front gate. It was a very small one, quite black, fluffy and round-eyed.

'I'll have to take that kitten back into its house, or it will be run over!' thought Donald, and began to run. But someone else had seen it too – the dog across the road. Ha – a kitten to chase! What fun!

And across the road sped the dog, barking. The kitten was terrified, and tried to run up a nearby tree – but it wasn't in time to escape the dog, who stood with his forepaws on the trunk of the tree, snapping at the kitten's tail and barking.

'Stop it! Get down!' shouted Donald, racing up. 'Leave the kitten alone!'

The dog raced off. Donald looked at the terrified kitten, clinging to the tree-trunk. Was it hurt?

He picked it gently off the tree and looked at it. 'You poor little thing – the dog has bitten your tail – it's bleeding. Whatever can I do? I'll just take you into the house nearby and see if you belong there.'

But no – the woman there shook her head. 'It's not *our* kitten. I don't know who it belongs to. It's been around for some time, and nobody really wants it. That's why it's so thin, poor mite.'

'What a shame!' said Donald, stroking the frightened little thing. It cuddled closer to him, digging its tiny claws into his coat, holding on tightly. It gave a very small mew.

'Well – I'd better take it home,' thought Donald. 'I can't possibly leave it in the street. That dog would kill it if he caught it! But whatever will Mother say? She doesn't like cats.'

He tucked it gently under his coat and walked home, thinking hard. What about that old tumble-down shed at the bottom of the garden? He could put a box there with an old piece of cloth in it for the kitten – and somehow he could manage to make the door shut so that it would be safe.

'You see, your tail is badly bitten,' he said to the kitten, whose head was now peeping out of his coat. 'You can't go running about with such a hurt tail. I'll have to get some ointment and a bandage.'

Donald thought he had better not take the kitten into the house. There might be a fuss. So he took the little thing straight to the old shed at the bottom of the garden. He saw an old sack there and put it into a box. Then he put the kitten there, and stroked it, talking in the special voice he kept for animals – low and kind and comforting. The kitten gave a little purr.

'Ah – so you can purr, you poor little thing! I shouldn't have thought there was a purr left in you, after your fright this morning!' said Donald. 'Now I'm going to find some ointment and a bandage – and some milk perhaps!'

He shut the shed door carefully, and put a big stone across the place where there was a hole at the bottom. Then he went down to the house. 'Is that you, Donald?' called his mother. 'Dinner will be ready in ten minutes.'

Ten minutes! Good! There would be time to find what he wanted and go quickly back to the shed. He ran into the kitchen, which was empty – his mother was upstairs. Quickly he went to the cupboard where medicines and ointments were kept, and took out a small pot and a piece of lint.

Then he took an old saucer, went to the larder, and poured some milk into it. He tiptoed out of the kitchen door into the garden, thankful that no one had seen him.

Up to the old shed he went. The kitten was lying peacefully in the box, licking her bitten tail.

'I wouldn't use your rough little tongue on that sore place,' said Donald. 'Let me put some ointment on it. It will feel better then. Perhaps it's a good thing, really, you've licked it – it's your way of washing the hurt place clean, I suppose. Now, keep still – I won't hurt you!'

And very gently, he took the kitten on to his knee and stroked it. It began to purr. Donald dipped his finger into the ointment and rubbed it gently over the bitten place. The kitten gave a sudden yowl of pain and almost leapt off his knee!

'Sorry!' said Donald, stroking it. 'Now keep still while I wrap this bit of lint round your tail, and tie it in place.'

The kitten liked Donald's soft, gentle voice. It lay still once more, and let the boy put on the piece of lint – but when he tied it in place, it yowled again, and this time managed to jump right off his knee to the ground!

Donald had put the saucer of milk down on the floor when he had come to the shed, and the kitten suddenly saw it. It ran to it in surprise, and began to lap eagerly, forgetting all about its hurt tail.

The boy was delighted. He had bound up the bitten tail, and had given the kitten milk – the two things he had come to do. He bent down and stroked the soft little head.

'Now you keep quiet here, in your box,' he said. 'I'll come and see you as often as I can.'

He opened the door while the kitten was still lapping its milk, shut it, and went up the garden. He was happy. He liked thinking about the tiny creature down in the shed. It was his now. It was a shame that nobody had wanted it or cared for it. What a pity his mother didn't like cats! If she had loved it, it could have had such a nice home.

'I'll have to find a home for it,' he thought. 'I'll get its tail better first, and then see if I can find someone who would like to have it!'

The kitten drank a little more milk, climbed back into its box, sniffed at the lint round its tail, and went sound asleep. Sleep well, little thing – you are safe for the night!

CHAPTER 3

A JOB FOR DONALD

It was not until the next morning that Donald found a chance to slip down to the shed to see the kitten. He took some more milk with him, and a few scraps.

'It will be so hungry!' he thought. 'What a good thing I left it some milk!'

But the milk had hardly been touched, and the kitten was lying very still in its box. It gave a faint mew when Donald bent over it, as if to say, 'Here's that kind boy again!'

'You don't look well, little kitten,' said Donald, surprised. 'What's the matter? You haven't lapped up the milk I left!'

He knew what the matter was when he saw the kitten's tail. It was very swollen, and the tiny creature had torn off the bandage with its teeth! It was in pain, and looked up at the boy as if to say '*Please* help me!'

'Oh dear — something has gone wrong with your poor little tail!' said Donald. 'Perhaps the wound has gone bad, like my finger did when I gashed it on a tin. *Now* what am I to do with you?'

The kitten lay quite still, looking up at Donald. 'I can't take you indoors,' said the boy. 'My mother doesn't like cats. I think I'd better take you to the vet. You needn't be frightened. He's an animal doctor, and he loves little things like you. He'll make your tail better, really he will!'

'Mew-ew!' said the kitten, faintly, glad to see this boy with the kind voice and gentle hands. It cried out when he lifted it up and put it under his coat.

'Did I hurt your poor tail?' said Donald. 'I couldn't help it. If we go quickly I'll have time to take you to the vet's as soon as he's there. It's a good thing it's Saturday, else I would have had to go to school.'

There were already three people in the vet's surgery when Donald arrived — a man with a dog, whose paw was bandaged; a women with a parrot that had a drooping wing; and a small girl with a pet mouse in a box. One by one they were called into the surgery — and at last it was Donald's turn.

The vet was a big man with big hands — hands

that were amazingly gentle and deft. He saw at once that the kitten's tail was in a very bad state.

'It was bitten by a dog,' said Donald. 'I did my best – put ointment on and bound it up.'

'You did well,' said the vet. 'Poor mite! I'm afraid it must lose half its tail. It's been bitten too badly to save. But I don't expect it will worry overmuch at having a short tail!'

'Perhaps the other cats will think it's a Manx cat,' said Donald. 'Manx cats have short tails, haven't they?'

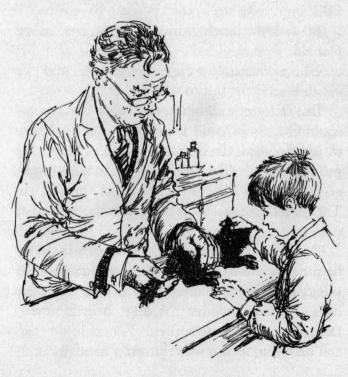

The vet smiled. 'Yes. Now you'll have to leave the kitten with me, and I must deal with its tail. It will be quite all right. It won't be unhappy here.'

Donald liked the vet very much. His big hands held the kitten very gently, and the little thing began to purr.

'Do all animals like you, sir?' he asked.

'Oh yes – animals always know those who are their friends,' he said. 'That kitten knows *you* are its friend. It will let you handle it without fear. I'll keep it for a week, then you can have it back.'

'Er – how much will your bill be?' asked Donald.

'Oh, *you* needn't worry about that!' said the vet. 'I'll send the bill to your father.'

'But, sir – my father and mother don't know about the kitten,' said Donald. 'You see – I kept it in my shed. It isn't mine, it's a stray. My mother doesn't like animals very much – especially cats. I'd like to pay your bill myself, sir. The only thing is – I haven't much money just at present.'

'Well, now, would you like to earn a little, by helping me?' said the vet. 'You could pay off the bill that way! My kennel-maid is away for a few days – she looks after the dogs here for me – feeds them and brushes them. *You* could do that, couldn't you, for a few evenings?'

'Oh YES! Yes, I could,' said Donald, really delighted. 'I'd *love* to. But would you trust me to do the job properly, sir? We've never had a dog at home. But I love dogs, I really do.'

'I'd trust any boy with any animal here, if he handled a kitten as gently as you do,' said the vet. 'It isn't everyone who has the gift of understanding animals, you know. You're lucky!'

'My Granny says that anyone who loves animals understands them,' said Donald.

'She's right,' said the vet. 'Now look – I've more patients waiting for me, as you saw. Leave the kitten in that basket. I'll attend to it as soon as I can. Come back tonight at half-past five, and I'll introduce you to the dogs. Right?'

'Yes, sir,' said Donald, joyfully, and put the kitten gently into the basket on the floor. Then out he went, very happy.

The kitten would be all right now. He could pay the bill by taking the job the vet offered him – and what a job! Seeing to dogs – feeding them – perhaps taking them for walks! But wait a bit – what would his parents say?

He told his father first. 'Daddy, the vet wants a boy to help him a bit while his kennel-maid is away,' said Donald. 'I thought I'd take the job – it's in the evenings – and earn a bit of money. You're always saying that boys are lazy nowadays – not like when you were young, and went out

235

and earned money even while you were at school.'

'Well! I didn't think you had it in you to take a job like that!' said his father. 'I'm pleased. So long as you don't neglect your homework, you can help the vet. Well, well – and I thought you were such a lazy young monkey!'

Donald was delighted. He could hardly wait for the evening to come! Looking after dogs! Would they like him? Would he be able to manage them? Well – he would soon know!

CHAPTER 4

DONALD GOES TO WORK!

Donald could hardly wait for the evening to come. He did his usual Saturday jobs – ran errands for his mother, cleaned his father's bicycle and his own, and weeded a corner of the garden.

Then his mother called him. 'What's this I hear from your father about your working for the vet? You know he's an *animal* doctor? You'll come home all smelly and dirty!'

'I shan't, Mother,' said Donald, in alarm. 'Goodness me, you should see the vet's place – as clean as our own! Anyway, Dad says it will be good for me.'

'Well, if you *do* come home smelling of those animals up at the vet's place, you'll have to give up the job,' said his mother. 'Fancy *wanting* to go and work with animals! I'm surprised at your father letting you!'

Donald kept out of his mother's way all day, really afraid that she would forbid him to go up to the vet's house that evening. He put on his very oldest clothes, and, when at last the clock said a quarter-past-five, off he went at top speed on his bicycle. His first job! And with dogs too! How lucky he was!

He arrived at the vet's, put his bicycle in a shed and went to find the kennels The vet was there, attending to a dog with a crushed paw.

'Ah – you're here already, Donald!' he said. 'Good – you're early, so you can give me a hand with this poor old fellow. He's had such a shock that he's scared stiff. I want to calm him down before I do anything.'

'What happened?' asked Donald, shocked to see the poor, misshapen front paw of the trembling dog.

'It was caught in a door,' said the vet. 'Apparently the wind slammed the door shut, and he couldn't get his paw away in time. He's a nervy dog. Do you think you can hold him still while I examine the paw?'

'I don't know. I'll try,' said Donald. He stroked the dog and spoke to it in his 'special' voice – the one he used for animals. 'Poor old boy – never mind – you'll soon be able to walk on that paw. Poor old boy, then, poor old boy.'

The dog turned to him, pricked its ears, and

listened. Then it licked Donald on the cheek, and gave a little whine of pain.

'Go on talking to him,' said the vet. 'Don't stop. He's listening to you. He won't mind about me if you take his attention.'

So Donald went on talking and stroking, and the dog listened, trying to get as close to the boy as he could. This boy was a comforting boy. This boy had a lovely, clean, boy-smell. He was worth listening to!

The dog gave a little whine now and again as the vet worked on his hurt paw. Soon the vet spoke to him. 'Nearly over now, old dog. I'm putting a plaster on, so don't be afraid. You'll be able to walk all right, your foot will be protected. Nearly over now.'

The dog gave a huge sigh and laid his head on Donald's shoulder. Donald was so happy to feel it there that he could hardly speak to the dog for a moment. He found himself repeating what the vet had said. 'Nearly over now, old dog, nearly over now.'

'Well – that's it,' said the vet, standing up. 'Come on, old dog – to your kennel, now, and a nice long sleep.'

The dog followed him, limping. Donald went too. The dog licked his hand every now and again, as if thanking him. The vet put him into a roomy kennel with straw on the floor, and shut the door. 'Goodnight, old dog!' called Donald, and from the kennel came a short bark – 'Woof-woof!'

'He'll be all right,' said the vet. 'You did well to hold him, youngster – a big dog like that. You have a good voice for animals, too. Now, here are the dogs I want you to brush, and to give fresh water to. Clean up any kennels that need it. You'll find fresh straw yonder if necessary.'

Donald had never had such an interesting

evening in all his life. There were five dogs in the kennels, each in a separate one – and all the dogs were different! He looked at them carefully.

'An alsatian – a labrador – goodness, he's fat – and a corgi with stubby little legs. He looks very intelligent. What's this dog, over in the kennel corner – a little black poodle – what a pet! And this last one – well, goodness knows what it is – a real mixture. A bit of a terrier, a bit of a spaniel, and a bit of something else!'

The dogs barked with joy when the boy came to them. They loved company of any sort and were longing for a walk.

'Three of them are here because their owners are away from home,' said the vet. 'The corgi has a bad ear. The little mongrel ate something he shouldn't and nearly poisoned himself, but he's feeling better now. You won't be scared of going into their kennels, will you? Their bark is worse than their bite!'

'Oh *no*, sir, I'm not scared!' said Donald. 'Shall I take them for a walk when I've finished?'

'Not tonight – we're a bit late,' said the vet. 'I'll take them out myself, last thing. You get on with the brushing.'

He left Donald alone. The boy was too happy for words. He had five dogs to see to – five! And what was more, they all seemed as pleased to see him, as he was to see them!

'Hello, all of you!' he said. 'I'm just going to fetch a can of fresh water for you. Then I'll clean out your kennels, put down fresh straw, and have a word with each of you. Shan't be long.'

And off he went, whistling loudly, to the tap he saw in distance. He filled a large can with water, and went back to the dogs. They were whining and barking now, the bigger ones standing with their paws on the top of their gates.

'I like you all very much,' said Donald, in his 'special' voice. 'I hope you like me too.'

'Woof-woof, WUFF, whine-whine, WOOF-WOOF!' Yes, they certainly liked Donald, no doubt about that. WOOF!

CHAPTER 5

A WONDERFUL EVENING

Donald had a wonderful evening with the five dogs. He went first into the labrador's kennel – it was rather like a small shed with a half-door or gate at the front, to get in by, fastened with a latch on the outer side.

The labrador was a big dog, a lovely golden colour. He stared at Donald in silence as the boy went in. 'Hello!' said Donald. 'How are you? Sorry I don't know your name. I've brought you some fresh water, and I'll sweep out your kennel and give you some fresh straw. Will you like that?'

The labrador lumbered over to the boy and sniffed his legs and hands. Then he wagged his tail slowly. Donald patted him. 'Are you home-sick?' he said. 'Poor old boy! Do you miss your master?'

At the word 'master' the labrador pricked up

his ears and gave a little whine. Donald emptied out the water-bowl, wiped it round with a cloth he had found by the tap, and poured in fresh water. The labrador lapped it eagerly. He didn't like stale water – this was lovely and cold and fresh! He sniffed at Donald again, decided that he liked him, and licked his bare knee.

Donald patted him, delighted. 'Sorry I can't stay long with you,' he said. 'I've the other dogs to see to. But I'll be back to give you a brush-down when I've finished.'

He went to the alsatian's kennel next. This too was a big one, almost a shed. 'Hello!' said Donald. 'My word, you've a big water-bowl – you must be a thirsty dog! Hey, don't drink out of the can, Greedy! That's right – you've plenty in your bowl! I'll come back again soon and brush you.'

The alsatian stopped drinking and went to his gate with Donald, hoping to get out and have a run. 'No, old boy,' said Donald, firmly. 'You'll have to wait for your walk till the vet takes you out tonight. Hey, let me get out of the gate!'

He went to the poodle next, a dear little woolly-coated thing that danced about on tiptoe as soon as the boy came into her kennel. She licked Donald everywhere she could.

'I shall have to bring a towel with me when I come to see *you*,' said Donald. 'You really have a *very* wet tongue. Now – drink your water. I'll be back again in a minute!'

The other two dogs, the corgi and the mongrel, were not feeding very well, especially the corgi, whose ear was hurting him. They wagged their tails and whined when Donald went in to them. The mongrel was very thirsty and drank all his water at once. Donald patted him.

'You're thin,' he said. 'And you look sad. I'll bring your some more water when I come in to clean your kennel.'

The mongrel pressed himself against the boy's legs, grateful for attention and kindness. He whined when Donald went out. That was a nice boy, he thought. He wished he could spend the night with him. He would cuddle up to him and perhaps he would feel better then!

The next thing was to clean out the kennels, and put in fresh straw. Once more the dogs were delighted when Donald appeared, and gave him loud and welcoming barks.

The vet, at work in his surgery, looked out of the window, pleased. The dogs sounded happy. That boy had made friends with them already. Ah, there he was, carrying a bundle of straw!

Donald cleaned out each kennel and put down fresh straw – and the five dogs nuzzled him and whined lovingly while he was in their kennels. He talked to them all the time, and they loved

that. They listened with ears pricked, and gave little wuffs in answer. They gambolled round him, and licked his hand whenever they could. Donald had never felt so happy in all his life.

He had to brush down each dog after he had cleaned the kennels, and this was the nicest job of all. The dogs really loved feeling the firm brushing with the hard-bristled brush. Each dog had his own brush, with his name on it, so to the dogs' delight, Donald suddenly knew their names, and called them by them!

When he had finished his evening's work, he patted each dog and said goodnight. All five dogs stood up with their feet on their gates, watching him go, giving little barks as if to say, 'Come back tomorrow! Do come back!'

'I'll be back!' called Donald, and went up to the surgery to report that he had finished. The vet clapped him on the shoulder and smiled.

'I've never heard the dogs so happy. Well done. Tomorrow is Sunday. Will you be able to come?'

'Oh yes — not in the morning, but I could come in the afternoon and evening, if you've enough jobs for me, sir!' said Donald. 'I'll be glad to earn enough money to pay off the bill for the kitten! Could I see the kitten, sir? Is its tail better?'

'Getting on nicely,' said the vet. 'I've got it in the next room. Come and see it.'

So into the next room they went, and there, in a neat little cage, lying on a warm rug, was the kitten. It mewed with delight when it saw Donald, and stood up, pressing its nose against the cage.

'It only has half a tail now,' said the boy sadly. 'Poor little thing. Is it in pain still?'

'Oh no – hardly at all,' said the vet. 'But I must keep it quiet until the wound has healed.'

'What will happen to it?' asked Donald. 'Nobody will want a kitten with only half a tail, will they? I *wish* my mother would let me keep it.'

'Don't worry about that,' said the vet. 'We'll find a kind home for it. You've done a good evening's work. Come along tomorrow, and you can take the dogs for a walk. I really think I can trust you with the whole lot!'

Donald sped home in delight. As soon as he arrived there, he rushed upstairs, ran a bath for himself, and then put on clean clothes. 'Now Mother won't smell a doggy smell at all!' he thought. 'I just smell of nice clean soap! But oh, *I* think a doggy smell is lovely! I can't wait till tomorrow, I really can't!'

CHAPTER 6

SUNDAY AFTERNOON

Donald was very hungry for his supper. He had really worked hard that evening. His mother was surprised to see the amount of bread and butter that he ate with his boiled egg.

'What's made you so hungry?' she asked. 'Oh, of course – you've been helping the vet, haven't you? What did you do?'

'I cleaned out the dog kennels – five of them,' said Donald. 'And I . . .'

'Cleaned out dog kennels! Whatever next?' said his mother, quite horrified.

'Well, I emptied the water-bowls and put in fresh water – and I brushed-down an alsatian called Prince, a labrador, a corgi, a poodle and a mongrel!' said Donald. 'May I have some more bread and butter, please?'

His father began to laugh. 'Boil him another egg, bless him,' he said. 'He's worked harder at the vet's this evening than he ever does at school. It's something to know that he can work well, even if it's just with dogs, and not with books.'

'Well, these dogs are jolly interesting!' said Donald. 'Dad, you should have seen how they all came round me – as if they'd known me for years!'

'That's all very well,' said his mother, 'but I do hope you won't forget your weekend homework in your excitement over these dogs.'

'Gracious! Homework! Oh blow it – I'd forgotten all about it!' said Donald, in dismay. 'It's those awful decimal sums again. I wish I could do sums about *dogs* – I'd soon do those! And I've an essay to write about some island or other – dull as ditch-water. Now, an essay about *dogs* – I could write pages!'

'Just forget about dogs for a bit and finish your supper,' said his mother. 'Then you really must do a little homework.'

'I'm tired now. I'd get all my sums wrong,' said Donald, yawning. 'I'll do it tomorrow morning, before we go to church. I'm going to the vet's again in the afternoon and evening.'

'My word – you *are* keen on your new job!' said his father. 'I'm pleased about that. But I shall stop you going if your school-work suffers, remember.'

Poor Donald! He really was tired that evening

after his work with the dogs. He couldn't do his sums properly. His head nodded forward and he fell asleep. It was a good thing that his parents had gone out! When he awoke it was almost nine o'clock! He hastily put away his undone work and rushed up to bed, afraid that his parents would come in and find his homework still not done.

'I'll have time in the morning!' he thought.

'I'll set my alarm clock and wake early. My mind is nice and clear then!'

So, when his alarm went at seven, he leapt out of bed, and tackled his sums. Yes – they *were* easier to do first thing in the morning. But oh that essay! He'd do that after breakfast. But after breakfast his mother wanted him to do some jobs for her – and then he had to get ready to go to church. That silly essay! What was the sense of writing about something he wasn't at all interested in? If only he could write about those five dogs! Goodness, he would be able to fill pages and pages!

He had told the vet that he would be at the surgery at half-past two. That left him just twenty minutes after midday dinner to do the essay! He took his pen and wrote at top speed, so that his writing was bad and his spelling poor, for he had no time to look up any words in the dictionary.

He looked at the rather smudgy pages when he had finished. His teacher would *not* be pleased. Oh dear – he really hadn't time to do it all over again. Maybe he could wake up early next morning and rewrite it!

Donald changed quickly into his old clothes and rushed out to get his bicycle. Then away he went, pedalling fast, glad that no one had stopped him, and asked him to do a job of some sort!

The boy had a wonderful afternoon. The vet took him into an airy little building where he kept birds that had been hurt, or were ill – and budgerigars that he bred himself for sale. Donald was enchanted with the gay little budgies. The vet let them out of their great cage, and they flew gaily round Donald's head, came to rest on his shoulder or his hand – and one even sat on his ear!

'Oh, how I'd love to breed budgies like these!' he said. 'How I'd like a pair for my own!'

'Good afternoon,' said a voice, suddenly, almost in Donald's ear. 'How are you, how are you, how are you?'

Donald looked round in surprise – and then he laughed. 'Oh – it's that parrot talking!' he said. 'A lovely white parrot! Is he hurt, or something?'

'No. I'm just keeping him for a time because his owner is ill,' said the vet. 'He's a wonderful talker!'

'Shut the door! *Do* shut the door!' said the parrot, and Donald obediently went to the door! The vet laughed.

'Don't shut it! It's just something he knows how to say – one of the scores of things he's always repeating!'

The parrot cleared its throat exactly like Donald's father did. Then it spoke again, in a very cross voice. 'Sit down! Stand up! Go to bed!'

Donald began to laugh – and the parrot laughed too – such a human laugh that the boy was really astonished. Then the vet took him to a shed where he kept any cats that needed his help. The little kitten was there too, curled up asleep, its short tail still bandaged. It looked very happy and contented. There were four big cats there also, one with a bandaged head, one with a leg in plaster.

'All my patients,' said the vet, fondling one of them. 'Cats are more difficult to treat than dogs – not so trusting. Mind that one – she's in pain at the moment, and might scratch you!'

But before the vet had even finished his sentence, Donald was stroking the cat, and talking to it in his 'special' voice. It began to purr loudly, and put down its head for him to scratch its neck.

The vet was amazed. 'Why, that cat will hardly let even *me* touch it!' he said. 'Look, I have to change its bandage now – see if you can hold the cat quiet for me, will you? It fought me like a little fury this morning. Will you risk it? You may be well and truly scratched!'

'I'll risk it,' said Donald, happily. 'I love cats and kittens. Show me what to do, sir – how to hold her. Hark at her purring! *She* won't scratch me!'

Be careful, Donald. Cats are different from dogs. If you go home with your face scratched and torn, you won't be allowed to go and help the vet again. So do be careful.

CHAPTER 7

DONALD IS VERY BUSY

'What's the matter with the cat, sir?' asked Donald, as he went on fondling the nervous animal.

'It's hind legs somehow got caught in a trap,' said the vet. 'One has mended well, but the other is badly torn, and won't heal. So I have to paint the leg with some lotion that stings – and this the cat can't bear!'

'How did you manage to hold the cat, and deal with its leg at the same time?' asked Donald, as the cat began to stiffen itself in fright. 'Did the kennel-maid hold it for you when she was here?'

'Oh no – she was frightened of the cat,' said the vet. 'It's half-wild, anyhow – lives in the woods. The keeper brought it to me. It's a lovely cat, really – half Persian. Now – can you hold it. I'll show you how to.'

Gently the vet took the cat and showed the boy how to hold it for him. The cat suddenly spat at him and tried to leap away, her claws out. But the vet's hold was firm and kind.

'I see, sir. I see exactly.' said Donald. 'Poor old puss, then. Don't be scared. We're your friends, you know. Poor old Puss.'

'Go on talking to the cat,' said the vet. 'It's listening to you just like that hurt dog did. You've a wonderful voice for animals. Many children have, if only they knew it – it's a low, kind, soothing voice that goes on and on and animals can't *help* listening. Go on talking to the cat, Donald. It's quieter already.'

The cat struggled a little as Donald held her, talking smoothly and quietly in his 'animal' voice. Soon she lay limp in his hold, and let the vet do what he pleased with her bad leg. She gave a loud yowl once when the lotion suddenly stung, but that was all.

Soon the bandage was on again, and the cat lay quietly in Donald's arms, purring. 'Shall I hold her for a bit, sir?' said the boy. 'She sort of wants comforting, I think.'

The vet looked at the boy holding the wounded cat. 'You know, son, you should be a vet yourself when you grow up!' he said. 'You could do anything with animals! They trust you. How'd you like to be an animal-doctor?'

'I'd like it more than anything in the world!' said Donald. 'I love animals so much — and they love me, sir! They do, really. I've never had a real pet of my own — my parents aren't fond of animals — so I've always had to make do with caterpillars and a hedgehog or two, and once a little wild mouse . . .'

'And I don't suppose you were allowed to bring them into the house, were you?' said the vet. 'Well, some people like animals and everything to do with nature — and some don't. We're the lucky ones, you and I, aren't we?'

'Yes. We are,' said Donald, carrying the cat back to its cage. 'It's not much good my thinking of being an animal-doctor, though, sir. I think I've got to go into my father's business and be an architect. And the awful thing is, I'm no good at figures or drawing or any of the things that architects have to do. I shall be a very, very bad architect and hate every minute. And I shall keep dozens of stray animals in my backyard, just to make up for it!'

The vet laughed. 'If you want a thing badly enough, you'll get it,' he said. 'You'll be a vet one day, and be as happy as the day is long! Now to work again!'

Donald spent a very happy Sunday at the vet's. He helped him with more of the animals, he cleaned out the birds' cages, and, best of all, he took all the five dogs for a long, long walk!

The vet telephoned his parents to ask them if Donald could stay to tea with him, so he didn't need to rush home at half-past four. He went to fetch the dogs, calling 'Who's for a walk, a WALK, a WALK!' They all began to bark in delight, and the alsatian did his best to jump right over the top of his high kennel-gate!

'Take them on the hills,' said the vet. 'There will be few people there, and you can let them loose for a good run. Whistle them when you want them to come to you. *Can* you whistle, by the way?'

Donald promptly whistled so long, loudly and clearly, that the vet jumped – and all the dogs in the kennels began to bark in excitement!

'Watch out for the corgi when you're on the hills,' said the vet. 'He may not be able to keep up with the others, on his short legs. And don't lose the mongrel down a rabbit-hole – he's a terror for rabbits.'

Donald set off happily, with the five dogs gambolling round him. They might have known him for years! Once on the hills they galloped about in joy. The mongrel promptly went half-way down a rabbit-hole, and Donald had to pull him out!

A man came walking down the hill towards them. Prince, the alsatian, immediately went to

sniff at him, and the man shouted at him 'Go away!' and struck out with his stick. The big alsatian growled at once, showing all his fine white teeth.

'Call your dog off!' yelled the angry man to Donald – and the boy suddenly stopped in astonishment. Goodness – it was Mr Fairly, his schoolteacher. He whistled to the alsatian, and the dog returned to him at once – and so did the other four! They all ran to him at top speed, and milled round him in delight, whining for a pat.

Mr Fairly was astounded to see Donald – the dunce of the maths class – with five gambolling dogs! 'What in the world are you doing with this army of dogs!' he yelled. 'That alsatian's dangerous!'

'He's all right, sir!' yelled back Donald, quite pleased to have seen his fierce maths master scared of a dog. 'I'm taking them all for a walk. Heel, boys, heel!'

And, to the master's astonishment, every dog obediently rushed to Donald's heels, and walked behind as meekly as school children. Well, well – the boy might not be able to do sums – but he could manage dogs all right! What a very surprising thing! There must be more in that boy than he had ever imagined!

CHAPTER 8

DONALD GETS
INTO TROUBLE

In the week, Donald could only manage to go to the vet's in the evenings – and how he looked forward to the time after tea when he could slip off to the kennels and see to the dogs. They welcomed him with barks that could surely be heard half a mile away!

But poor Donald had a shock when Wednesday arrived, and the essays of the week-end came up for correction. He had handed in his smudgy, hastily written one, ashamed of it, but not having had enough time to do it again.

Mr Fairly his form master had the piles of essays in front of him, and dealt with the good ones first, awarding marks. Then he looked sternly at Donald, and waved an exercise book at him – Donald's own book!

'This essay must be written all over again!' he said. 'In fact, I'm almost inclined to say it should be written out *three* times. The spelling! The handwriting! The smudges! Donald, you should be in the lowest form, not this one! I am really ashamed to have a boy like you in my class.'

'I'm sorry, sir. I – well – I had rather a lot to do in the weekend,' said poor Donald.

'Ha yes – taking out dogs for a walk on the hills, I suppose!' said Mr Fairly. 'Well, I shall ask your parents if they will please see that your homework is done – and done well – before you go racing off with the most peculiar collection of dogs that I have ever seen!'

'Oh please, sir, don't complain to my parents!' said Donald. 'I'll rewrite the essay, sir. I'll – I'll write it out *three* times if you like!'

'Very well. Rewrite your essay three times tonight, and hand it in tomorrow,' said Mr Fairly. 'I fear, Donald, that that will mean five dogs will have to do without your company after tea!'

'The mean fellow!' thought Donald, angrily. 'He must *know* I am taking the vet's dogs walking after tea – and that's about the worst punishment he could give me – making me sit indoors, writing essays when he knows I love walking the dogs!'

But there was nothing to be done about it – Donald had to tell the vet he wouldn't be up after tea that day.

'Bad luck,' said the vet, kindly. 'The dogs will miss you. Never mind. Just come when you can. I'll manage.'

Donald sat down after tea to rewrite his essay. Blow, bother, blow! What a waste of a lovely evening! Would the dogs miss him? Would they be looking out for him? What a pity he couldn't write about *them*, instead of rewriting his stupid essay!

His mother was astonished to find him in his bedroom, writing so busily. 'I thought you would be up at the vet's,' she said. 'Are you doing extra homework, or something?'

'Well – sort of,' said Donald. His mother looked closely at what he was doing, and frowned.

'Oh Donald! You're rewriting an essay! And no wonder! *What* a mess you made of it – however could you give in work like that? I suppose you wrote it in a hurry because you give up so much time to helping the vet.'

'The weekend was so busy,' said Donald, desperately. 'I just had to hurry over my essay.'

'Well, you know what Daddy said – you can only go to help the vet if your school-work is good,' said his mother. 'I'm afraid you mustn't go any more.'

Donald stared at his mother, his heart going down into his boots. Not go any more? Not see those lovely dogs – and help with the cats and the birds? Not be with the vet again, the man he admired so much?

'I *must* go to the vet's,' he said. 'He's going to pay me for my work. I want the money for something.'

'What for?' asked his mother, astonished.

Donald looked away. How could he tell her that he had taken that little kitten to the vet's to be healed and looked after, so that he might perhaps have it for his own pet, hidden away somewhere? How could he tell her that what he earned at the vet's was to pay for the kitten's treatment? She didn't like cats. So how could she understand what he felt for the tiny kitten that had been chased and bitten by a dog?

But it was all no good. His mother told his father about his badly written essay, and he agreed that if Donald's work was poor because he hadn't enough time for it, then of course he must give up helping the vet. And what was more, he telephoned the vet himself, and told him that Donald was not coming any more.

The vet was very sorry. He liked Donald – he liked the way he did his work with the animals – he would miss him. And what about that little kitten? Well – he must find a good home for it. A pity that boy had no pets of his own – he was marvellous with animals!

Donald was very unhappy. He missed going to the vet's. He missed the companionship of all the animals, so friendly and lively. He began to sleep badly at nights.

One night he lay awake for hours, thinking of

the five dogs, the cats – and the little kitten with the half-tail. He wouldn't be able to see the kitten any more – and he somehow couldn't help feeling that it ought to belong to *him*.

He sat up in bed, and looked out towards the hill where the vet lived. 'I've a good mind to dress and go up to the kennels,' he thought. 'The dogs will know me – they won't bark. They'll be very glad to see me. *They* don't mind if I'm no good at sums or essays. I'm quite good enough for *them*. They think I'm wonderful. I'm not, of course – but it *is* so nice to be thought wonderful by *some*body!'

He dressed quickly, and slipped quietly down the stairs. He let himself out by the back door, locking it after him, and taking the key in case any burglar should try to get in.

'Now for the dogs!' he thought, feeling his heart lighter already. 'They'll be so surprised and pleased! I'll feel better after I've been with them for a little while. Oh dear – sometimes I think that dogs are nicer than people!

CHAPTER 9

IN THE MIDDLE
OF THE NIGHT

Donald wheeled his bicycle quietly out of
the shed, and was soon speeding along
the dark roads, and up the hill to where the vet
lived. 'I'll just have half-an-hour with the dogs,'
he thought. 'I'll feel much better when I've had a
word with them, and felt their tongues licking
me lovingly.'

He was soon at the familiar gate, and rode in
quietly. He put his bicycle into an empty shed,
and went towards the kennels. Would the dogs
bark, and give the alarm, telling the vet that
someone was about in the night? Or would they
know his footsteps, and keep quiet?

The dogs were asleep – but every one of them
awoke almost as soon as Donald rode into the
drive! Prince, the big alsatian, growled – and
then, stopped, his ears pricked up. A familiar
smell came on the wind to him – a nice, clean

boy-smell – the smell of that boy who looked after him a week or so ago! The alsatian gave a little whine of joy.

The corgi was wide awake too, listening. He didn't growl. He felt sure it was the kind boy he liked so much. He tried to peer under his gate, but all he could see was the grass outside. Then he heard Donald's voice, and his tail at once began to wag.

Soon Donald was peering over the gates of the dogs' kennels. The alsatian went nearly mad with joy, but gave only a small bark of welcome, for Donald shushed him as soon as he saw him.

'Sh! Don't bark! You'll wake the vet. I'll come into each of your kennels and talk to you. I've missed you so!'

He went first into the alsatian's kennel, and the dog almost knocked him over, in his joy at seeing him. He could not help giving a few small barks of delight. He licked the boy all over, and pawed him, and rubbed his head against him. Donald stroked and patted, and even hugged him.

'It's so lovely to be with you again,' he said. 'I've missed you all so. I'm in disgrace, but *you* don't mind, do you? Now, calm down a bit – I'm going to see the other dogs. I'll come and say goodbye to you before I go!'

He left the alsatian's kennel and went to the

next one. The corgi was there, his tail wagging nineteen to the dozen, his tongue waiting to lick Donald lovingly. The boy hugged him and tickled him and rolled him over. The corgi always loved that, for he had a great sense of fun.

Then into the next kennel, where the little poodle went nearly frantic with joy. She leapt straight into his arms, and covered his face with licks. She had missed him very much. Donald sighed happily. What a lot of love dogs had to give!

Then out he went, and into the next kennel belonging to the mongrel dog. He had gone nearly mad when he had heard Donald in the other kennels, talking to the alsatian, the corgi and the poodle. He threw himself at the boy, and began to bark for joy.

'Sh!' said Donald, in alarm. 'You'll wake everybody, and I'll get into trouble. SHHH!'

The mongrel understood at once. He was a most intelligent dog, as mongrels so often are, and he certainly didn't want to get Donald into trouble. He calmed down, and contented himself with licking every single bare part of Donald he could find – knees, hands, face and neck!

'I do wish I'd thought of bringing a towel with me,' said Donald, wiping his face with his hanky. 'Now calm down – I'm going to see the labrador next door to you!'

But when he shone his torch into the next kennel, the labrador wasn't there. Another dog was there, a beautiful black, silky spaniel, the loveliest one that Donald had ever seen. He shone his torch on her, and she gave a little whine. She didn't know Donald. Who was this strange boy that all the other dogs seemed to welcome so lovingly?

'Oh – the labrador's gone back home, I suppose,' said Donald, disappointed. 'But what a lovely little thing *you* are! And oh, what have you got there – tiny puppies! Let me come in and see them. I promise not to frighten them.'

The spaniel listened to the boy's quiet voice and liked it. She gave a small whine as if to say, 'Well, come in if you like. I'm proud of my little family!'

So Donald opened the gate and went in. The spaniel was a little wary at first, but Donald knew enough of dogs to stand perfectly still for a minute while she sniffed him all over, even standing up on her hind legs to reach to his chest. Then she gave a tiny bark that meant 'Pass, friend. All's well!' and licked his right hand with her smooth tongue.

She went to her litter of tiny puppies and stood by them, looking up as if to say, 'Well? Aren't they beautiful?'

'Yes, they are. And so are you,' said Donald, stroking the smooth, silky head of the proud spaniel. 'You must be the very, very valuable spaniel that the vet told me was soon being sent to him. He said you are worth a hundred and fifty pounds, and that your puppies would be worth a lot of money, too. Oh, I wish I'd been here when you came, and could have looked after you, and cleaned your kennel and given you water.'

The spaniel curled herself round her litter of puppies, and looked up happily at Donald. He gave her one last pat. 'Goodnight. I'll leave you in peace with your little black pups.'

He went out of the kennel and saw the alsatian still standing with his paws on the top of his kennel-gate, listening for him. 'I'll just come in again and keep you company for a little while,' said the boy, and, to the dog's delight, he went into the kennel and sat down in the straw beside the big dog.

He laid his head on the dog's shoulder, and Prince sat quite still, very happy. It was warm in the kennel, and quiet. Don't go to sleep, Donald! Your eyes are shutting. Wake up, Donald, someone's coming! *Wake up!*

CHAPTER 10

A SHOCK FOR DONALD!

Donald was fast asleep. He was warm and comfortable and happy. The big alsatian kept very still, glad to feel the sleeping boy so near him, his ears pricked for the slightest sound. He felt as if he were guarding Donald.

Suddenly he began to growl. It was a very soft growl at first, for he did not want to disturb the boy. But soon the growl grew louder, and awoke Donald.

'What is it? What's the matter?' he asked Prince, who was now standing up, the hackles on his neck rising as he growled even more fiercely. Then he barked, and the sudden angry noise made Donald jump.

'What's up?' he said. 'For goodness sake don't bring the vet out – he may not like my coming up here at night!'

But now the alsatian was barking without

ceasing, standing up with his feet on the gate, wishing he could jump over it. A stranger was about, and the great dog was giving warning!

'I'd better go,' thought Donald. 'If the vet comes and finds me here, he may think it was I who disturbed the dogs. Gracious, they're *all* barking now! Can there possibly be anyone about? But why? No thief could steal one of these dogs – they would fly at him at once!'

The corgi was barking his head off, and so was the mongrel dog. Even the little poodle was yapping as loudly as she could. Only the black spaniel was quiet. Perhaps she was guarding her puppies, and didn't want to frighten them?

Donald climbed over the alsatian's gate, afraid that if he opened it, the great dog would rush out, and it might be very, very difficult to get him back! He was amazed to see somebody coming out of the *spaniel's* kennel gate! There was very little moon that night, and all the boy could see was a dark figure, shutting the gate behind him.

'There's two of them!' said Donald to himself, as he saw someone else nearby. 'What are they doing? Good gracious, surely they can't be stealing the spaniel's puppies? Where's my torch? I must go to her kennel at once!'

The two dark shadows had now disappeared silently into the bushes. Donald took his torch from his pocket and switched it on. He ran to the spaniel's kennel and shone the light into it.

'The spaniel's still there,' he thought, 'Lying quite still as if she's asleep. I'd better go in and see if all her puppies are beside her.'

So in he went, and shone his torch on to the sleeping dog. Alas, alas – not one single puppy was beside her! She lay there alone, head on paws, eyes shut.

'How can she sleep with all this row going on, every single dog barking the place down!' thought Donald. 'She must be ill!'

He touched the dog – she was warm, and he felt her breath on his hands. He shook her. 'Wake up – someone has taken your puppies! Oh dear, those men must have knocked you out! They were afraid you'd bite them, I suppose! Wake up!'

But the spaniel slept on. Donald stood up and wondered what to do. The thieves had a good start now – he wouldn't be able to catch them. But wait – he knew someone who *could* trail them – someone who wouldn't stop until he had caught up with the wicked thieves!

He rushed back to the alsatian's kennel. The dog was still barking, as were all the others. 'Prince, Prince, you're to go after those men!' shouted Donald, swinging open the great gate. 'Get them, boy, get them! Run, then, RUN!'

The great alsatian shot off like an arrow from a bow, bounding along, barking fiercely. He disappeared into the darkness, the trail of the thieves fresh to his nose. Ah – wherever they had gone, wherever they hid, the alsatian would find them!

Donald suddenly found his knees shaking, and he felt astonished. 'I'm not frightened! I suppose it's all the excitement. Oh, those lovely puppies! I do hope we get them back!'

And then somebody came up at a run, and caught hold of him. 'What are you doing here? Why have you roused the dogs! You deserve to be scolded!'

It was the vet! He couldn't see that the boy he had caught was Donald. He gave him a good shaking, and Donald fell to the ground when he had finished.

'Don't, sir, don't!' he cried, struggling up. 'I'm Donald, not a thief. Sir, thieves have been here tonight and have stolen the spaniel's puppies, and . . .'

'What! Those wonderful pups!' shouted the vet, and rushed to the spaniel's kennel. He shone a powerful torch there. 'I must get the police. I heard the dogs barking, and came as soon as I could. But what on earth are *you* doing here this time of night?'

'I couldn't sleep so I just came up to be with the dogs,' said Donald. 'I know it sounds silly, but it's true. I've missed them so. And I fell asleep in the alsatian's kennel, and only woke up when the thieves came. They got away before I could do anything.'

The vet shone his torch in the direction of

Prince's kennel. 'The door's open!' he cried. 'The dog's gone!'

'Yes. I let him out, to go after the thieves,' said Donald. 'You told me once that alsatians are often used as police dogs – for tracking people – and I thought he *might* catch the thieves.'

'Donald – you're a marvel!' said the vet, and to the boy's surprise, he felt a friendly clap on his back. 'Best thing you could have done! He'll track the thieves all right – *and* bring them back here. I wouldn't be those men for anything! Now – we'll just ring up the police – and then make ourselves comfortable in Prince's kennel – and wait for him to come trotting up with those two wicked men! Ha – they're going to get a very – unpleasant – surprise!'

CHAPTER 11

GOOD OLD PRINCE!

It was very exciting, sitting in Prince's kennel in the dark, waiting for the alsatian to come back. The vet and Donald were not the only two waiting there – two burly policemen were there also!

The vet had telephoned to the police station and the sergeant and a policeman had cycled up at once, as soon as they heard what had happened. 'Good idea of that boy's, to send the dog after them,' said one man. 'Very smart. Wish *I* had a dog like that!'

The other dogs were awake and restless, especially the spaniel, who missed her puppies, and whined miserably. The men in the alsatian's kennel talked quietly, and Donald listened, half-wondering whether this could all be a dream. Then suddenly the mongrel gave a small, quiet bark.

'That's a warning bark,' said the vet, in a low tone. 'Shouldn't be surprised if Prince has found those men already, and is on his way back with them.'

Soon the other dogs barked too, and the two policemen stood up, and went silently into the dog-yard. The vet and Donald stood up too. The boy felt his knees beginning to shake with excitement again. He heard a fierce growl not far off, and a sharp bark. Yes – that was Prince all right! And what was that groaning, stumbling noise?

'That's my dog coming,' said the vet, 'and by the sound of it, he's got the men. I can hear them stumbling through the wood. I only hope they've brought back the pups.'

As the stumbling footsteps grew nearer, the police moved forward, and shone a powerful torch into the nearby bushes. The beams picked out two terrified men – and a great dog behind, his teeth bared, and a continuous growl coming from his throat – Prince, the alsatian! He had followed the trail of the men for a mile – and caught up with them! How frightened they must have been when he rounded them up!

'Stand where you are!' said the sergeant's voice, sharply. 'You're under arrest. Where are the puppies?'

'Look here – that brute of a dog has bitten

me!' said one of the men, holding out a bleeding hand. 'I want a doctor.'

'You can wait,' said the sergeant. 'A police van will be up here in a few minutes, and I'll take you down to the police station, both of you. Where are the puppies?'

'We don't know,' said the other man, sullenly. 'We dropped them when we found this dog chasing us. Goodness knows where they are!'

'That dog's a dangerous one,' said the other man, eyeing Prince carefully. 'He nipped my friend too – on the leg.'

'Serves you right,' said the vet. 'Look, sergeant, I've *got* to find those pups, or they'll all die. They need their mother. Will you see to these men, and I'll go off with Prince and see if he can find the pups for me.'

'May I come too?' asked Donald, eagerly.

'Yes. You may as well see this night's adventure to the very end!' said the vet, taking the boy's arm. 'He's done well, hasn't he, sergeant?'

'My word he has!' said the man. 'Pity he's not in the police force! Maybe you will be some day, young fellow.'

'I shan't,' said Donald. 'I'm going to be a vet. I could train police dogs for you then, if you like!'

That made everyone laugh. Then the vet gave the boy a little push. 'Come on, old son – we've got to find those puppies within an hour or so, or we may lose one or two of them – they'll be scared, and very hungry. Prince! Go find, Prince! Find my spaniel puppies.'

The black spaniel, still wide awake, was surprised at all the noise, and sad at the loss of her tiny puppies. She suddenly gave a sharp bark. 'She says she wants to come too,' said Donald.

'Right. We'll take her,' said the vet, and the

little company set off through the bushes – first
Prince, the alsatian, then the vet with a basket,
then Donald, then the spaniel, nosing behind.

'How will Prince know where those men
threw down the puppies?' asked Donald, as they
went through the woods, the vet's torch throwing a bright beam before them.

'Well, he must have passed near them, when
he trailed those men,' said the vet. 'He'll remember all right. You can't beat an alsatian for tracking man or animal! Hi, Prince – don't go too
fast. The spaniel can't keep up with us!'

Prince went steadily on his way, standing still
at times to sniff the air. After he had gone about
half a mile he stopped. The spaniel gave an excited bark and ran forward.

'Prince has smelt the pups,' said the vet. 'So
has the spaniel. Don't go any further. Let her go
forward to them first.'

The spaniel forced her way through the under-
growth, barking excitedly. Then she suddenly
stopped and nosed something, whining in
delight. The vet shone his torch on her – and
there, in the grass, lay the puppies, every one of
them! The mother licked them lovingly, and
then looked up at the vet. She turned back and
tried to pick up one of the pups in her mouth.
She must carry it home!

'It's all right, old lady,' said the vet, in the

same special 'animal' voice that Donald so often used. 'It's all right. I've brought a basket, look – with a warm rug inside. You shall watch me put all the pups into it, and when I carry the basket you can walk back home with your nose touching it. They'll be safe – and you will soon be back in your kennel with them.'

And then off went a little procession through the dark woods. First, Prince, very pleased with himself. Then the vet with the basket of pups. Then the spaniel, her nose touching the basket all the time. And last of all a very happy, excited boy – Donald. *What* a night! And oh, *what* a good thing it was that he hadn't been able to sleep – and had slipped up to the kennels! Yes, Donald – that was very lucky. But you do deserve a bit of luck, you know!

CHAPTER 12

SURPRISE FOR DONALD

When the vet, Donald, and the dogs, at last arrived back at the kennels, the telephone was ringing. The vet sighed.

'I hope it's not someone to say they want me to go and look at a sick cat, or a moping monkey!' he said. 'It's still the middle of the night, and I'm tired. Aren't you, Donald?'

'I am a bit,' said Donald. 'But I don't mind. It's been – well, quite an adventurous night, hasn't it?'

The vet went to the phone. 'Hello? Yes. Who is it? Oh, Donald's father! Yes, actually, Donald *is* here. I'm sorry you were worried. Er – well, apparently he couldn't sleep, so he popped up to be with my dogs. Good thing he did, too. We've had an exciting night – been after thieves – and caught them too. Donald's been quite a hero. Well – the boy's tired out now. Shall I give him a bed for the night? Yes, yes – I'd be glad to have him. Right. Goodnight!'

'Gracious – was that Dad?' said Donald, alarmed. 'Was he very angry because I'd come up here in the middle of the night?'

'No. No, I don't think so,' said the vet. 'He seemed very relieved to know you were here, safe and sound. You get off to bed, old son. You can have the room next to mine. Don't bother about washing or anything – you're tired out. Just flop into bed.'

Donald fell asleep almost at once. He was tired out, as the vet had said, but very happy. What a good thing he had come up to the kennels – and had spotted those thieves! What a good thing that Prince had found those lovely little spaniel puppies! What a good thing that . . . but just then he fell fast asleep, and slept so very soundly that he didn't even stir until the vet came to wake him the next morning.

'Oh goodness – shall I be late for school?' said Donald, looking in alarm at his watch.

'No. Calm down. It's Saturday!' said the vet. 'Your mother's been on the phone this morning – she sounds very excited about something – I won't tell you what! She says will you please come back in time for breakfast.'

'Oh dear – I hope I'm not going to get into any more trouble!' said Donald, jumping out of bed.

'No, I don't somehow think you'll find trouble waiting for you!' said the vet. 'Buck up, though – and come back and help me today if you're allowed to.'

Donald dressed at top speed and shot home on his bicycle. Would his father be angry with him for slipping away in the middle of the night? Well – it had been worth it! It was a pity he hadn't been able to go and see if the spaniel puppies were all well and happy this morning, but maybe he could come back later on in the day.

He arrived home, put his bicycle away, and ran in through the kitchen door. Mrs Mawkins, the cook, called out to him as he came in.

'Oh there you are, Donald. Fancy you being in the papers this morning!'

Donald had no idea what she meant – but he soon knew! As soon as he went into the sitting-room, his mother ran to meet him and gave him a hug.

'Donald! Oh Donald, I didn't know I had such a brave son!'

'Well done, my boy!' said his father, and clapped him on the back. 'Fancy you being in the papers!'

Donald was astonished. He stared at his father, puzzled. 'What do you mean, Dad?'

'Well, look here!' said his father, and showed him the first page of his newspaper – and there,

right in the middle, was a paragraph all about Donald!

'Boy sends alsatian dog after thieves, in middle of night. Helps police to find priceless spaniel puppies.' And then came the story of how Donald had gone up to the kennels in the middle of the night, heard the thieves, sent the alsatian after them – and all the rest!

'I suppose the police told the paper all that last night,' said Donald, astonished. 'Mother, I couldn't sleep for thinking of those dogs, that's why I went up to them in the middle of the night. I know you and Dad said I wasn't to go and help the vet – but I did so want to see the dogs again. I just felt sort of lonely.'

'Well, all's well that ends well,' said his father, feeling really very pleased with Donald. 'Your mother and I are proud of you. We've been talking things over, and we're both agreed that you *shall* go and help the vet again . . .'

'Oh Dad! THANK you!' cried Donald, his heart jumping for joy. 'Now I'll be able to see those spaniel puppies again that the thief took. Oh, they're beautiful! Oh, I wish I was rich enough to buy one! Oh, and that little kitten too. I wish I was rich enough to pay the vet to keep it for me! I wish I could buy a . . .'

'Well now, that's enough, Donald,' said his father. 'It's no good getting big ideas, especially while your school-work is poor.'

'What about your homework for the weekend?' said his mother. 'You mustn't forget that, in all the excitement! What have you to do? Sums? An essay? Geography or history?'

'I've forgotten,' said Donald, feeling suddenly down-hearted. 'Bother it! Where did I put my exercise book? The homework I've to do for the weekend is written there. I don't feel *at all* like doing any!'

He fetched his exercise book and turned to the page where instructions for his weekend home-work were written down. 'Here it is – oh blow, an *essay* again! '*Write down what you would like to be when you grow up, and give the reasons why.*' Donald stared at it in sudden delight. 'Why – I can do *that!* I want to be a vet, of course – and I know *all* the reasons why. I can put dogs and cats and horses and birds and everything into *this* essay. I'll write it at once, this *very* minute!'

CHAPTER 13

A WONDERFUL DAY

It was really very surprising to see Donald settling down so very happily to do his homework. 'We usually have such silly, dull things to write about,' he said. 'Now *this* is sensible. I've plenty to say! I only hope there are enough pages to say it in.'

It was while Donald was finishing the longest essay in his life that there came a knock at the door. It was a man from another newspaper, wanting to ask questions about Donald and his exciting night.

'I'm sorry,' said his father. 'The boy has had enough excitement. We don't want him to talk to newspaper men, and get conceited about himself.'

'Oh, I only want to ask him a few questions,' said the man. 'Such as, what does he plan to be when he's grown up? Maybe a policeman, perhaps, catching robbers and the like?'

Donald, writing his essay, heard all this. He ran to the door. 'Why – that's *exactly* what I'm writing for my weekend essay!' he said, surprised. 'I'm going to be a vet, of course. I'm putting down all my reasons. I've just finished!'

'And what are your reasons?' asked the man, smiling at Donald.

'Now listen,' said Donald's father, pushing the boy away. 'We've told you that we don't want our son to think himself too clever for words, and to get conceited! The most we'll let you do is to read what he has written.'

'Let me just have a look at it, then,' said the man. Donald handed the exercise book to him and the man glanced quickly down the essay.

'Good, good, GOOD!' he said. 'Best essay I've read for ages – straight from the heart – you mean every word of it, don't you, youngster? Do you get top marks every week for your essays? You ought to.'

'No. I'm pretty well always bottom,' said Donald. 'But this is different. It's something I *like* writing about, something I *want* to write about. I know all about a vet's work, you see. It's *grand*.'

'Go away now, Donald,' said his father, anxious not to let the boy talk too much. 'Leave your essay with me.'

Donald went off, and his father turned to the

waiting newspaper man. 'You can have this essay of his, instead of talking to him, if you like. But I think you should pay the lad for it, you know, if you want to print it. I'll put the money into the bank for him.'

'Right. Here's five pounds,' said the man, much

to the astonishment of Donald's father. 'And if that form master of his marks him bottom for *this* essay, well, all I can say is, the man doesn't know his job! I'll take it with me, have it copied, and send back the essay in time for him to take it to school next week. Thank you, sir. Good-day!'

And away went the man, looking very pleased with himself. 'Ha!' he thought, 'fancy that kid writing such an interesting piece about a vet's work, and all his animals — most remarkable! Good boy that. Deserves to have animals of his own. Funny there wasn't even a dog about the place — or a cat! Well, maybe the five pounds would help him to buy a pet for himself!'

Donald's mother and father were very proud and pleased to have been given five pounds for his essay. They went to tell Donald.

'Good *gracious*! Five pounds for a school essay!' said the boy, astounded. 'I wish I'd written it better. It isn't worth ten pence, really. And I bet I'll be bottom in class as usual! But I *say — five pounds*! Now — what shall I spend it on?'

'Well — I shall put it in the bank for you, of course!' said his father. The boy stared at him in dismay.

'Oh *no* Dad! I want to *spend* it — spend it on something I badly want! It's *my* money. Mother, please ask Daddy to let me have it.'

'Yes. Yes, I think you *should* have it, dear,' said

his mother, very proud of all that Donald had done the night before. 'Give it to him, Dad – we'll let him spend it on whatever he likes. He shall choose!'

'Whatever I like, Mother – do you *really* mean that?' cried Donald. 'You won't say no to *any*thing?'

'Well – you've been such a brave lad, quite a hero – and I think for once you should do as you please,' said his mother.

'Mother – if I buy a puppy with it, will you say no?' asked Donald.

'I'll say *yes*, you deserve one,' said his mother, and his father nodded his head too.

'And – suppose I asked you if I could have a little hurt kitten that the vet's keeping for me – would you mind?' asked the boy. 'It has only half a tail, because a dog bit it, so it's not beautiful – but I do love the little thing. That's really why I went to work for the vet – because he took the kitten and tended it, and kept it – and when he said he would send the bill to Dad, I said no, I'd work for him, and he could keep my earnings to pay for the kitten.'

His mother suddenly put her arms round him and gave him a warm hug.

'You can have a dog, a cat, a kitten, a monkey, anything you like! We didn't know quite what a clever son we had, nor how brave he is. We know better now. We're very very proud of you, Donald.'

'Oh *Mother*! A dog of my own – a kitten! Oh, and I might get a donkey, if I save up enough. He could live in the vet's field. And I'll buy a cage and keep budgies – blue ones and green ones. Oh, I can't believe it!'

'And if Mr Fairly, that form master of yours, gives you low marks for that fine essay, I'll have something to say to him!' said Donald's father. 'Well, well – I suppose we must now give up the idea of your being an architect when you grow up, Donald. It will be fun to have a vet in the family, for a change! I'm proud of you, son – I really am!'

CHAPTER 14

DONALD – AND HIS DOG!

Donald's father kept his word. He didn't put the five pounds into the bank – he gave it to Donald. 'Gracious – how rich I am!' said the boy, delighted. 'Mother, do you mind if I go up to see the vet – and tell him about the money?'

'Off you go!' said his mother. 'But please come back for dinner – I'm going to arrange a very special one for you!'

Donald shot off to the vet's on his bicycle. He whistled as he went, because he felt so happy. To think that last night he was so unhappy that he couldn't even go to sleep – and today he was too happy for words! All because he rushed off to see the dogs in the middle of the night!

The vet was delighted to see him again so soon – and whistled in surprise when he saw the five pound notes that the boy showed him.

'Well, well – writing must be a paying job, if you can earn five pounds for an essay!' he said. 'It takes me quite a time to earn *that* amount!'

'Sir, would you please sell me one of those beautiful spaniel puppies?' said Donald, earnestly. 'I want one more than anything in the world. A dog of my own – just imagine! Someone who'll understand my every word, who'll always know what I'm feeling and will never let me down, because he will be my very faithful friend.'

'Well, if ever a boy deserved a dog, it's you, Donald,' said the vet. 'But I'm not going to let you buy one of those pups, I'll *give* you one. I meant to, anyway, for what you did last night, and for all the help you've given me. You shall choose your own pup. Come along – let's see which one you want, before anyone else has their pick.'

Donald was speechless. His face went bright red, and the vet laughed. 'Can't you say a single word? And there's another thing – that little kitten is well enough to go now – I know you want her. You can have her too. Let her and the pup grow up together.'

'Thank you, THANK YOU!' said Donald, finding his tongue. 'But please, I've plenty of money now! I can pay for them both.'

'I know. But if you really *are* going in for animals, you'll want kennels and cages and things,' said the vet. 'I'll show you how to *make* them – much cheaper than buying them – all you'll have to do is to buy the wood and the nails. You're good with your hands – you'll enjoy making things.'

'It all seems rather like a dream,' said Donald, as they went to look at the puppies. 'I was so miserable yesterday – and today I feel on top of the world! Oh I say, aren't the puppies *lovely*? They seem to have grown since last night. That little fellow is trying to crawl!'

The spaniel's mother looked up at them out of beautiful brown eyes. With her nose she gently pushed one of the puppies towards Donald. 'That's the one she wants you to have!' said the vet. 'It's the best of the lot.'

And that is the one Donald chose. He left it with the mother till it was old enough to be his – and now he is making a fine kennel for it! 'It will be yours when you are old enough,' he tells the puppy. 'I expect the kitten will sometimes sleep in your kennel with you, so I'll bring her along soon so that you can make friends.'

He went to tell his Granny about the dog he had chosen. She listened, very pleased. 'Well, well – I meant to give you a puppy myself, for your birthday, if your mother said yes – and now you have won one for yourself, by working for the vet. You deserve a dog, Donald, and I know you'll train him well. I can't give you a dog, now you have one – so I think I'll buy you a really good dog basket, so that you can have him in your room at night, to guard you when you're asleep!'

'That puppy is going to be very lucky!' said Donald. 'I'm making him a *lovely* kennel – the vet's helping me. We went and bought the wood together, out of the money I won for that essay. I've a kitten too – the one whose tail was half-bitten off by a dog. And I *think* I'm going to breed budgerigars, Granny. I've still enough money out of my five pounds to buy a breeding-cage. I'm going to give *you* my first baby budgie. Would you like a green or a blue one?'

'Oh – a green one, I think,' said Granny. 'It will match my curtains! Bless you, Donald – you do deserve your good luck. You earned it yourself – and that's the best good luck there is!'

Donald still goes up to help the vet, of course, and you should have seen him one week when the vet was ill! He looked after all the dogs, the cats, the birds – and a little sick monkey! How happy and proud he was! How good it felt to go round and see every animal, big or small, look up in delight when he came . . . Yes, Donald – you'll be a fine animal-doctor, when the time comes!

Prince, the alsatian, has gone back to his own

home now, of course – but Donald often sees him when he goes out. Prince always sees him first, though! Donald suddenly hears a soft galloping noise behind him – and then he almost falls over as the big alsatian flings himself on the boy, whining and licking, pawing him lovingly.

'Do you still remember that exciting night in the dark woods?' says Donald, ruffling the thick fur round the dog's neck. 'Remember those little spaniel puppies? Do you see this beautiful black spaniel at my heels – he was one of the pups we rescued that night, you and I! I chose him for myself. *Dear* old Prince. I'll never forget you!'

One day you may meet a boy walking over the grassy hills somewhere – a boy with five or six dogs round him, dogs that come at his slightest whistle. It will be Donald, taking out the kennel-dogs for the vet, letting them race and leap and play to their hearts' content. Call out to him – 'DONALD! Which is *your* dog?'

But you'll know which it is without his telling you – that silky black spaniel beside him. What's its name? Well, call 'Bonny, Bonny, Bonny' and it will come rushing over to you at once!

Goodbye, Donald. Goodbye, Bonny. Good luck to you both. You deserve it!